The Sundials of
Heart Island

The Sundials of Heart Island

Time travel is possible when
love forshadows the future.

VICKIE HODGE HOLT

authorHOUSE®

AuthorHouse™
1663 Liberty Drive
Bloomington, IN 47403
www.authorhouse.com
Phone: 1-800-839-8640

ROB MAHAN   (The Sundial In The Garden)
MATTHIAS KOHOUT   (Heart Island)

First published by AuthorHouse   12/08/2011

ISBN: 978-1-4670-3789-1 (sc)
ISBN: 978-1-4670-3788-4 (ebk)

Library of Congress Control Number: 2011916859

Printed in the United States of America

Chapter 1

"For the first time, I present to you, Mr. and Mrs. Rodger Calvert," Pastor Lewis announced to the wedding congregation.

Caroline and Rodger's lips, still warm from their first husband and wife kiss, whispered, "I love you". They turned to face their family and friends and the romantic glaze over their faces changed. Even through the oohs, ahhs, and clapping Rodger focused on the only person standing. A man in his mid to late sixties was leaning against the back wall, on the bride's side. Rodger did not recognize him, but his police training came natural, even at the altar.

The guest's two white-knuckled fists clutched an aged briefcase against his chest.

Rodger looked at all the happy faces before turning to observe his beautiful bride, Mrs. Caroline Calvert.

Her eyes, too, were examining the stranger. She turned to look into her husband's eyes and the mysterious guest was forgotten.

As soon as Rodger and Caroline reached the last pew, the stranger stepped forward and tapped his beefy finger in the center of his briefcase, which he was still clutching to his chest.

Rodger nodded, excusing himself to walk around the uninvited wedding guest. With Caroline on his arm, they exited to pose with the wedding party for photos.

It wasn't until everyone was reentering the empty sanctuary of Solid Rock Church that he saw the husky elderly man sitting on the back pew. Once the photographer had finished the wedding shots, everyone gathered at the fellowship hall for the reception. The stranger, with briefcase in tow, watched Rodger and Caroline as they interacted with each guest. Rodger noticed that the man acted more like an outsider. He did not talk to anyone there, and he avoided the receiving line.

He did make it to the cake table. "Twice," Rodger thought. "Today I am the happiest groom this world has ever seen, not an investigator!" Rodger scolded himself. Turning to feast his eyes on his beautiful bride, he let out a little chuckle when he followed her gaze to the seated stranger. He was eating wedding cake atop the makeshift table, the old briefcase.

When Caroline realized Rodger was watching her, she turned and adjusted the rose pinned to his tuxedo. "Scent One", Caroline swooned out his nickname, "A bud for a badge. Sweet! I like it. I love you." Rodger sniffed the rose, and smiled at Caroline, taking in her beauty.

"Each time I look into your eyes I see our love blossoming. I love you Rosebud."

Words the florist in Caroline fully grasped. For a tough investigator, Rodger remained clueless to the fact that he had it bad.

They would soon discover what it meant to bloom where you are planted.

Someone snapped a photo of the expression on Caroline's face the moment she saw what 'someone' had done to Rodger's car. Final photos of the newlyweds were taken as cheers and tears flowed from family and friends.

Five miles from the church, Rodger realized the 'briefcase man' was following them in a white windowless van.

Caroline released her seat belt and scooted next to Rodger. That gave her access to the rearview mirror. Glancing up, Caroline looked into the windshield of the van Rodger seemed so interested in.

"Caroline, was he your guest?" Rodger asked.

"I've never seen him in my life. I take it you don't know him, either," Caroline answered, never diverting her eyes from the rearview mirror.

When Rodger pulled into the next gas station, the van pulled in behind them. Before Rodger could think about getting out of the honeymoon mobile, the man with his briefcase, still against his chest, bolted from his van to the driver's window, on Rodger's side. Rodger pressed the down button, ripping away some crepe paper. The men glared at each other in silence.

With a lunge, the briefcase landed on the hood of Rodger's car. Shaking, liver-spotted hands carefully lifted a manila package from the briefcase. When he slammed the briefcase closed, both Rodger and Caroline jumped.

Each thought; *a wedding gift*?

"Thank you for stopping. My name is Emanuel Bishop. Take this with you," he said shoving the package onto Rodger's reluctant palm. "Read it ASAP. I think you might want to take a look at this before you head off on your honeymoon. The contents could change your plans. There is a map inside, the deed, and several keys. My business card is also inside. You have some papers to sign, but that can be done when you return, if you return."

With that, the stranger abruptly stood from his bent position, looked all around the area, and then stealthily returned to his van. Caroline watched through the rearview window as the briefcase, which was no longer at his chest, but rather, down by his side, easily sailed into the van's passenger seat.

Empty, she thought.

The newlyweds stared as the van sped away.

It was Caroline who spoke up first, "Did he say deed?"

Rodger, watching the van disappear replied, "I think so, Mrs. Calvert. My first act as your husband is to go to our apartment and look inside this envelope." Rodger noticed his knuckles were white from gripping the package.

"I agree, husband," Caroline slowly whispered, "Let's go."

Chapter 2

With the key still inside the deadbolt lock of their new apartment, Rodger froze. With a sly grin on his face, he turned and locked his gaze on his bride. It took a moment, but it finally registered.

Caroline giggled as she raised her arms to fit around Rodger's neck, all the while holding onto the package.

Effortlessly Rodger hoisted his bride into his arms and carried her over the threshold. As soon as he set her down, they kissed. When they realized they both had their eyes open looking at the mysterious package, they laughed at each other.

"It's a good thing we got married. We saved two other souls from being out of whack somewhere in this world", Caroline could have quoted those words. Rodger was always pointing out how in-sync they responded.

They walked in the kitchen and plopped the package on the kitchen table.

"Well, this is not exactly how I envisioned our honeymoon starting off, but please have a seat in the new kitchen chair we are supposed to find when we return from our trip." He pulled out a chair and with a one-handed sweeping motion bowed as she sat.

"I hope you like it. Your brother insisted I choose the set", Caroline mused as she watched for Rodger's delightful smile. There it was. Perfect. Then both sets of eyes went down to the tabletop and gawked at the package. So far, it had already altered their plans and introduced them to a mysterious old man.

Caroline turned the package over and carefully pealed back the top. She slid a handful of paper out and then dumped the contents onto the table. A rather slender rectangular box, much like one that you might wrap a bracelet in, slid out first. Then a key ring landed with a jangle. It secured two long rusty keys and a silver butterfly locket.

Rodger chose the papers.

Caroline gently inspected the butterfly locket. After feeling the details engraved on the butterfly, Caroline reached for the long box. It had a rusty key inside filling the full length of the box. It looked like a skeleton key she remembered her grandmother having which opened the cedar chest at the foot of her bed. The top of the key resembled a sundial with ruts and grooves for numbers.

Rodger let out a sudden yelp. "Whoo Hoo! Caroline, we own a home! Sounds like a mansion. This is the deed to the house and land! Did you find two keys?" He was a bit loud inside their small apartment but his excitement could not be contained.

"Yea, there are three keys here. We own what?" Caroline set everything down so she could read along with Rodger.

He was absorbed, and fascinated by the *Last Will and Testament* of George Boldt.

Rodger placed the gold foil-edged stationary on the table and began reading each page aloud.

"On the day that Caroline Boldt weds, she and her husband are to inherit the mansion, theater, gardens, and lands of the entire estate of George Boldt. The address is Heart Island, New York. The island is located in the Saint Lawrence Seaway, in the United States of America. It is the desire of Boldt that she and her husband live in the mansion for one year (three-hundred and sixty-five days) before the deed is placed in their names. At that time, the estate fully belongs to them to live in or to sell. If it is sold, all three structures on the property, and the gardens, must be destroyed. If they do not return, or decide not to take ownership of the estate, all must be destroyed. The mansion is to be demolished along with all of the botanical gardens. The deed will be donated to the city of New York and the vacant land will be used for whatever they desire. I would prefer a family park, or a botanical nursery be developed on

the property should said heirs forfeit their inheritance. Being of sound mind and body, this is the last request of George C. Boldt.

Caroline's eyes were wider than the day Rodger had proposed marriage. She did not realize she was actually holding her breath. A gasp came out. "A mansion? Botanical gardens?"

She was still gasping for air.

"Weird. Way too weird. Wait. There are . . . gardens. If I forfeit or refuse to live there a year, then whoever Boldt is wants a botanical nursery developed on the property. Weird! Rodger, that sounds like bait. I am a horticulturist! Why wouldn't I want the gardens in the first place?"

They snapped their heads to look at each other.

They slowly whispered into each other's stare, "W-e-i-r-d!"

It didn't take them long to snap back at the papers, bracing themselves for further instructions.

"Wait! Caroline, who is Boldt?" Rodger thought Caroline might have heard of the name, since she was adopted.

"I have no idea." Caroline said shrugging her shoulders as she looked at the keys on the table.

More questions began to form on Rodger's lips. He did not want to sound like a cop doing an interrogation. Determined not to begin their marriage with secrets, he loosened the bow-tie around his tightening throat. He would approach this as a caring, loving, husband.

"Darling wife, did you read the part that said, 'If we do not return'?"

Rodger waited for an answer.

"That is the second time we've been handed that challenge today. Once was from the weird old man and now in print. Scent One, do you think that is a threat, or a challenge?" Caroline moved her eyes to study Rodger's face.

"This just went from weird to spooky. I say we grab all this stuff and head out to the airport and switch our tickets. What do you think, Rosebud?" Rodger knew the answer even before he asked.

"We just inherited a mansion for crying out loud! I can't wait to see the gardens! Let's go on an adventure. It is about time we had a little fun. We just got married!"

With a wink, they scooped everything into the package, and fled their new apartment.

Chapter 3

Rodger fearlessly typed away on his laptop while Caroline drove the highly noticeable crape-paper-wrapped, "Just Wed" escape car to the airport. Thanks to the Wi-Fi connections, the plane tickets were changed and it was New York or bust. The new plans were a go!

Solving a mystery inheritance, an island, and some rusty old keys would get any cop's attention.

The gardens were a temptation to the newly graduated horticulturist.

The ride to the airport was all but silent. Rodger was wondering if anyone knew the details surrounding his wife's adoption.

Caroline was wondering about her real parents. "Rodger, you would think I would have at least thought of my maternal mother today, but I haven't. Not until I heard the word "inherited", at least. Do you think I should call Mama and Daddy and tell them about this?" Caroline's eyebrows scrunched together as she drove and awaited Rodger's reply.

"I do. Maybe they can tell you something about your adoption that they haven't already told you. It would be nice to know who Boldt is, or was. If you will honk and wave at the kids admiring the decorations on my freshly-waxed car I'll hand over the cell phone." Rodger crawled half of his lean body across the passenger headrest and unzipped his carry-on bag to retrieve his cell phone.

Caroline's conversation with her adoptive parents failed to shed any light on the subject. They had never heard of Boldt, nor had any idea how New York could possibly have anything to do with

Caroline's past. Her parents wished them well and warned them to be careful and not to sign any papers until their lawyer had a chance to go over them.

They all agreed.

They only had a thirty-minute wait with the newly arranged plane tickets. Just enough time to use the laptop to cancel the other honeymoon suite reservations.

They truly were on an adventure. They could not help but giggle as they boarded the plane.

After they adjusted their seat belts, Rodger lifted travel magazines from the seat pocket in front of him.

"Caroline", Rodger nudged as he pointed to a picture in an ad, "look at these resorts. Maybe when we see the mansion and its gardens we won't want to come back." Rodger knew as he said this that the references could not have meant they might change their minds about returning.

So what did it mean?

Like clockwork, Caroline shot a glance into her husband's eyes that said she was thinking the same thing.

Exactly what was the meaning of *if they returned*?

After changing planes, twice, their plane began its descent to the New York runway.

Rodger felt like a true explorer as he replaced the last tourist magazine. He found the perfect place for their honeymoon. It had a romantic garden designed for strolls and a luncheon area with swings and a butterfly garden. All things he knew Caroline would adore and remember for years. Rodger got his laptop out of his briefcase to make the reservations.

The honeymoon suite was available. They were on an adventure, all right.

Caroline had been dozing when the reservations confirmed, so their new destination would be a surprise. As Rodger repacked the laptop, he checked under Caroline's feet to make sure her bag was securely nestled under her feet.

"Habit," Rodger whispered to himself. He wondered how much was a habit-of-the-badge and which part was his new role as a husband. Watching Caroline's innocent face as she slept made him realize just how vulnerable she was, and how watchful he would always be.

"Some habits are good for a husband", he whispered into her hair as he lightly kissed the top of her head.

Before he gently awakened his bride to prepare for landing, he laughed at how he had done a background check on his shooting range partner's newest girlfriend.

Habit, yep, just a habit.

Chapter 4

Once the plane landed, the luggage loaded into the taxi, their mysterious getaway was now within reach. The joy of adventure in Caroline's eyes was better than all the teasing they had enjoyed while carefully planning their honeymoon. The suite, surrounded by gardens in full bloom, would be the perfect and most memorable retreat Rodger could have ever hoped to give his bride. As the taxi pulled to the curve, Caroline admired the cherry blossoms carved into the heavy wooden doors. They looked at the murals of gardens wrapping the front entrance.

Rodger carried Caroline across the threshold, set her on her feet, and kissed her passionately before looking into her eyes. She smiled up at him, and snuggled her face to his chest.

"I know dear, it is almost lunch time and you want to see the gardens, too." Rodger whispered as he held the love of his life.

Caroline nodded, keeping her sneaky grin to herself.

They quickly dropped their luggage in the doorway and locked their honeymoon suite, for later . . . much later.

"I love these gardens. I could live right here, if you would stay with me," Caroline said with twinkling eyes while she planted a sweet kiss on Rodger's chin. "You picked the perfect place for our honeymoon. I have to laugh though. We downloaded images, checked references, made several calls, and then canceled our reservation at the last minute. Those people must think we are quirky." Caroline said as she pulled Rodger along the garden's trail.

Hand in hand, they stopped to smell the flowers, admired the decoratively trimmed hedges, and sat on a hand-carved tree trunk so they could listen to the birds and animals that shared their hideaway.

Caroline sniffed at Rodger's shoulder and sputtered, "Yep, the "Scent One" I married is an adventurer."

Rodger pulled what looked like a remote control from his pants pocket and asked Caroline if she was ready for their picnic lunch.

"Make that, my 'high-techno adventurer'. Yea, Scent One, this is the perfect spot." Caroline was still glowing with joy as she watched Rodger press the buttons that would have their lunch catered to them.

"'Garden Gala' is what they call this service. I'm surprised we found a spot so isolated," Rodger put his arm around his wife as they leaned into each other and waited for their lunch to arrive.

"Rodger, do you remember the day you came into the florist shop and sneezed out your introduction?" Caroline blushed for them both.

"How could I forget, Rosebud? That was the best "God bless you" I have ever received. That was the first time I sneezed and my heart refused to start working again, until I asked you out on a date." Rodger slowly explained as he reminisced, planting a kiss on top of Caroline's head.

"Well, I have a confession to make about your nickname," Caroline eased the words out but avoided his gaze.

"Mrs. Caroline Calvert, did I have to marry you just to get a confession out of you?"

"No mister investigator! However, your nickname has a double meaning."

"Like a double agent?" quipped Rodger as he raised one eyebrow.

"Not exactly, my husband dearest. I called you Scent One because of all the sniffing you and your men did while trying to identify the flowers the peeping tom was leaving at that heiress's home. Your sneezes were so cute I had to pay attention to you. But, I didn't have to embarrass you any further! I referred to you as Scent One just to cover up the fact that I knew you were the one God had sent to me. My 'knight in shining badge', if you will."

Rodger bent double with laughter, sending his beauty into a straight position. He stood to gaze into her eyes.

Rodger belted out a big laugh and stuttered through his question.

"You actually liked my sneezing?"

"I felt sorry for you, that's all," Caroline used her words to balance the situation.

"Yea Rosebud, I see you are finally about to blossom!"

The newlyweds laughed together, sharing their love and joy. They giggled, again, when the waiter arrived and failed miserably at attempting to hide his grin.

"That waiter looked at us like we were the blooming idiots growing in the garden."

Rodger enjoyed one more laugh with his bride before diving into the picnic lunch.

After strolling through the butterfly garden, it was time for a little sightseeing. New York is a place of adventure and an excellent place to experience the history and birth of the nation. They both agreed it was a better choice than their persnickety plans that had taken hours to choose and only moments to terminate.

After dinning in their honeymoon suite, they decided not to unpack, but rather, tomorrow, to move closer to Heart Island. Tomorrow morning they would take the ferry ride from the banks of New York through the Saint Lawrence Seaway to Heart Island.

What would they find there? What did the keys in the envelope open?

Rodger knew he would look with his trained eye before they spoke to anyone. None else needed to know about the keys before scoping out the island, its buildings, and the gardens.

"*Mum's* the word, until we get a good look around," Rodger used the flower term to lighten the mood that seemed to settle upon each of them.

Caroline snickered at his play on words but knew all too well that he had every intention of guarding her identity and protecting their information, as well as those keys. They would hold each other, no matter what the day held for them.

"I've always known I was adopted. My adoptive parents are the only family I have ever known. I never felt like I didn't have a real family. I've thought about my maternal parents many times, but I figured if they hadn't provided information for me to be able to find them, then they must not have wanted a relationship with me. Rodger, when we said our vows I felt like we were starting our own family. But when Mr. Bishop called me an heir and I heard the name Boldt, I felt displaced for the first time in my life." Caroline had a faraway look as she tried to find words to explain her emotions.

Rodger wrapped his arm around his wife. He knew words would be inadequate. His touch was meant to provide all the security and love he could muster.

She read him well enough as she returned from her thoughts and nuzzled into his understanding embrace. Each newlywed moment drew them closer. This was a new way to communicate and they treasured their time alone.

Chapter 5

After touring the Big Apple, it was time to follow a different map; the map inside the manila envelope they had received on their wedding day. They made reservations to tour Heart Island. They decided to blend in with the tourists and learn what they could. The paddle boat ride was brief, but the fresh air and sunshine created a romantic atmosphere, charged with anticipation. The island was actually hewn into the shape of a heart.

There were three mansions on the island. A yacht house was the third on the brochure. There would be sixty vessels inside the yacht house, which had several doors opening to the seaway. Heart Island had become a tourist stop for New York. Anyone taking a voyage through the Thousand Islands might travel by way of yachts, smaller boats, or tenders from larger ships. Thousands visited the home built by the very wealthy George Boldt, for his lovely wife. The tour guide waited until everyone was off the white three-story paddle boat before he began to tell the story of Heart Island.

"On behalf of George, and Louise Boldt, welcome and watch your step", the muscular armed tour guide said in his well-practiced manner. The first two mansions were on the list for a quick tour. The tour guide introduced himself as Mr. Shane Hajji and led the way to the first rock-built mansion.

"This beautifully crafted mansion would make a fine home for any family. Would you like to move in today?" he asked the small crowd of about forty.

One young boy raised his hand and said, "My mama would like to live in a castle like that."

Everyone laughed, until Mr. Hajji opened the door.

"Inside you will find no tables, no chairs, and no kitchen." Mr. Hajji swept his upward palm forward indicating they should enter ahead of him.

The father of the little boy shouted out, "No kitchen? Oh, now I know your mother would love to move in today", again, the crowd laughed.

"Yes, but sir, there also are no homey luxuries like bathrooms," Hajji tried to finish.

The mother sputtered out making the crowd roar with laughter. "They are wrong! I won't move in until one of those is installed."

After waiting for the laughter to dissipate, Hajji continued, "This castle is housing the power generator for the entire island. You could say this is the home of the heart of Heart Island." Mr. Hajji moved aside to allow the line to look inside at the metal churning away, sound proofed by the rock-walled castle.

"I don't think we've seen the heart of this place yet." Rodger tried to speak over the sound of the generator as he puffed into Caroline's wispy strands of hair falling from her ponytail, hoping no one else could hear.

Caroline was not looking inside, nor was she listening to the deafening generator inside the rock covered castle. Her eyes closed, she was clearly inhaling the exotic aromas of the island.

Rodger whispered, "Rosebud," as he gently touched her shoulder. Her glazed eyes once again focused.

"Oh, sorry," She said as she shook herself back into reality. "Rodger, I can't believe the aromas blending with the ocean air. I wish Mr. Hajji would take us to the gardens. I'm more interested in the exotic blooms I smell than the mansions. I can't wait for you to see the colors. I already know three of my favorites are out there somewhere," she said as she exhaled, relaxing her lungs.

"Maybe I should call you the Scent One", Rodger teased as he took her by the hand, nudging her forward. They had to keep up with the crowd long enough to learn more details about the property, buildings, and of course, the gardens.

As they rounded a few azalea bushes, in full bloom, Rodger decided to end Caroline's suffering by simply asking. "Mr. Hajji",

Caroline shot Rodger a questioning look as he began, "At what point will you guide us through the gardens?"

"Ahh," Mr. Hajji replied, "You can smell their fragrances already," Caroline decided to answer that one.

"Oh, yes Mr. Hajji. It is almost intoxicating."

"Try not to get too high, Missy, we have a long way to walk yet." He laughed. "The gardens are the last treat on our agenda. We will have lemonade, cookies, and other refreshments in my favorite spot of the garden before we board the paddle boat."

Rodger was smiling at the thought of lemonade.

Caroline did not think she could wait that long.

"Rosebud," Rodger whispered into her ear, "Try to remember, this island belongs to us now. You can walk, inhale, and plant in these gardens all your little heart desires." Caroline's smile spread across her face as if she realized this to be true for the very first time. Caroline was thinking about pinching herself.

"Funny thing about reality, sometimes it doesn't seem real."

She could not seem to get that silly grin off her face, as she inhaled, and identified gardenias.

"This small castle is an elaborate playroom. George intended for Louise to invite their friends to share this beautiful island. This castle is *The Children's Play House*. Note it has three pointed castle tops, one for each of George's 'girls'. Louise personally shipped the heart-shaped ivy you see winding across the rock walls. Her ivy covers nearly half of the Play House today. It has twenty rooms as well as its own theater. The Boldts already had two daughters so everyone supposed he intended for the guests to 'getaway' from the main house and relax in a castle all their own. Today, honeymooners enjoy their stay here while capturing the view of the Saint Lawrence Seaway. You can see the yacht house on Fern Island from here. Please note the heart designs in the wrought iron every seven feet. Every room has a heart engraved into the mahogany headboards." Mr. Hajji paused so the tourists could admire the view and construction.

Rodger's eyes met Caroline's, and without a word, just a nod, they agreed they would spend the next few days in this honeymoon suite, if it were available to the owners.

Mr. Hajji began describing the castle as they walked up the main steps.

"In the year nineteen hundred, George C. Boldt began construction on this castle as a tribute to his enduring love for his wife Louise. This labor of love has one hundred and twenty-one rooms in thirty-five hundred square feet of luxury. You will see engraved ceiling moldings, a round motif in the stain glassed dome ceiling, red walls, hand-laid parquet flooring, and a marble hearth in front of the fireplace, which honors the family name with a beautifully engraved letter "B.""

During the construction, a normal workday consisted of three hundred hand-selected, skilled workers. Can you imagine walking into this home for the first time and seeing the labor of love your spouse created for your pleasure?"

Wives looked at each other and sighed, "Nooo . . . ," in unison.

Laughter escalated from the front porch as the tourists gathered. Mr. Hajji opened the two heavy hand-carved doors and swept his palm forward, jesting the crowd enter. Loud gasps echoed from the first to enter. Like a wave, the expressions of awe continued as anticipation rolled, gathering in the last of the tourists.

Rodger and Caroline gasped when the entrance came into view.

Awesome is not the word for it. It was like basking your eyes in a vacation of beauty. Rays of brilliant light shone down from the huge, round stained glass copula in the ceiling. Their eyes followed the four climbing, open banister-wrapped stairs, stretching upward, out of sight. The red walls made the flooring shine with a rich feel of warmth and stability.

Mr. Hajji led everyone around the first floor. "Ladies first," Mr. Hajji said as he led the group into a sitting room. "This is the ladies sitting room, the only room with wallpaper. Louise selected this pattern, herself." Hajji did not speak while the women entered, as if he knew he was out of place in the room intended for women.

The moldings where stunning, bold, and yet femininely intricate. Eyes, dreaming of romance, fell upon the heart carvings in the tall backs of the comfortable chairs. The beauty welcomed the women to a domain all their own. Prim and proper tea tables delicately invited ladies to sit, rest, and chat with friends while being served tea and cookies on the finest of imported china.

"Next, the men's billiard room," Mr. Hajji said, looking comfortable next to the pool table as he pointed out the game room.

Chocolate colored, bulky leather chairs were scattered throughout the room. The dining room walls were red and the floors shone with its mahogany wainscoting. There were fabric inlays, two brass chandeliers, and seven wall sconces, framed by ornate red mahogany ceiling beams fourteen feet above. A library, with glass-enclosed shelves, towered behind an oval leather covered desk.

Caroline thought how masculine it all looked. Caroline was running her finger along the top of the black leather chair, snugly fitting under the desk, when she noticed an oil painting over the fireplace. It was a somber faced man with Boldt's Castle painted in the background. There was a stark resemblance between Caroline and the man in the photo.

He was balding but the hair color in the beard looked like it might have matched the color of her own, when she was younger. Rodger could feel Caroline's heart through her expression. The wondering, the years of questioning her real heritage, were lodging in her throat as she looked at aged Boldt family photos. Behind her was a library with glass-enclosed shelves, which towered behind an oval leather covered desk. Elegance, charm, comfort, all things Caroline dreamed about and did without in the orphanage, and her adoptive parent's home.

The group, now completing the tour of the first floor, returned to the entrance. The stairs were gorgeous. Mr. Hajji climbed to the second step, stopped, and folded his arms until everyone was quietly watching him.

"I see you feel the same way I do every time I enter this castle. I hope you have a hanky," he said as he looked up the stairs.

"I never tire in my position as host of Boldt Castle." Everyone froze with anticipation, including Mr. And Mrs. Rodger Calvert. "When this castle was ninety-five percent finished, Louise passed away of a rare disease. George commanded all work to stop and three-hundred workers packed their tools and left this island.

George never returned to Heart Island. Fifty-two years later, and sixteen million dollars' worth of renovations, Heart Island's Boldt castle was opened to the public for tours and weddings."

Stillness was in the air, as if the tourist's hearts were suffocating from the emptiness and the loss.

"Please, enjoy thirty-minutes of exploring the home Louise never saw."

Gasps went out. No one seemed in a hurry to move from his or her spot.

The labor of one man's love was evident everywhere they looked.

Forgetting the gardens, their scents, and forgetting her part in all of this, Caroline looked at the empty halls and empty rooms that had never heard the playful giggles of two daughters.

For once, Rodger was wondering what she was thinking. Rodger was wondering how Caroline fit into the story that Mr. Hajji had just eloquently delivered.

As the crowd moved ahead, Caroline found herself thinking about the lineage of the Boldts. Where were the other descendants?

Was she the sole heir?

Who hired the attorney?

How did he know to show up on her wedding day? Caroline was looking at the beautiful details in the castle while her mind became more and more distracted and jumbled with unanswered questions.

Mr. Hajji cleared his throat rather loudly, getting the crowd's attention again.

"Before we step outside, please look above the fireplace as you exit. May I present to you the queen of Boldt Castle, Mrs. Louise Boldt?"

With that announcement, everyone turned around, following Mr. Hajji's glare, and pointed fingertips.

This time, Caroline gave the first gasp. Rodger's hand flew to his mouth with an audible slapping sound. It was clearly Caroline's face in a black and white photo.

A tourist standing next to Caroline tugged on her husband's sleeve and whispered something into his ear.

He turned and looked at Caroline, then at the photo. He widened his eyes at his wife, and they huddled close in a quiet conversation as they followed the crowd.

"As you pass by the fireplace, please note the marble inlaid flooring in front of the hearth. It is in the familiar shape of a heart and Mr. Boldt commissioned the letter "B" to be hand crafted inside the heart."

Caroline caught a glimpse of Rodger's face and knew 'the badge' was closing in on more questions.

Chapter 6

Finally! Finally! The gardens! There were several gardens. The air was intoxicating. With each breath, Caroline's mind drifted, following each diverse scent.

Mr. Hajji laughed aloud as he watched the tourists inhale and exhale.

"It never fails," he declared, "grownups acting like children. Go ahead; those bushes were groomed into mazes for your sheer pleasure. Romp, skip, explore, be a child again. Enjoy the flowerbeds. We will meet here at the iron-gate in fifteen minutes." Hajji shooed them away like children.

On cue, everyone scattered into the green mazes.

Caroline spotted a taller interest, above the hedges. In a stiff stance, Caroline's thoughts were almost detectable. A large, green, canvas-covered nursery was in the center of the gardens. Someone wanted the nursery disguised. Huge Leyland Cypress trees lined the entire structure. Scanning the area, Caroline's training revealed each displaced tree. A garden was no place to attempt to disguise something from Caroline.

In that moment, Rodger realized she could have been working for his team.

In fact, they were a team.

Once the newlyweds looked into each other's eyes, they confirmed the mystery brewing.

Time to roam!

Leaving the tour group was easy enough, but it would not be easy to swim back to the shores of New York should they miss the paddle boat.

Rodger was interested to hear where Caroline wanted to begin their adventure.

"What do you want to see first?" Rodger followed Rosebud away from the mazes and under the limbs of a Leyland Cypress. Hand in hand, they eased through the open door to the flourishing nursery. Neither could speak, at first. The nursery seemed empty of employees, but Caroline squeezed Rodger's fingers signaling him to wait a moment more. They stepped inside, both inhaling the damp earthy scent laden with the smell of exotic flowers. She pointed to an enclosed area, to the left, inside the nursery. Eyes wide, she gripped his wrist and tugged him through the second door. No one was there.

"Marvelous!" Caroline whispered. "This is a lab. Look at those beakers. That is one of the rarest Orchids in the world. They are growing them by using the plant's tissue culture and other plant material."

Rodger was not familiar with what they had stumbled on to, but he was amazed at her interest.

"Only a few labs do this kind of work. Why would anyone want to preserve or perhaps alter an Iris?"

Rodger knew better than to match wits with a highly acclaimed horticulturist, but he cross-examined her in his own way.

"I know these flowers are rare, but are they endangered, or extinct?" He hoped he did not sound too silly to the expert. She didn't respond, so it must have been silly, he reasoned.

Caroline gave the lab a quick scan. Sniffing again, Caroline recognized the scent of an Alaskan flower. Her ponytail flipped into her eyes when she quickly turned her head to find the Fireweed. Large sections of Fireweeds filled planters in neatly arranged rows. As Caroline made her way past several tables of herbs, Rodger could feel her anxiety and was in quick pursuit.

"They look like they are on fire. What are they? I've never seen anything like this, Caroline?" Rodger knew she would have an answer, this time.

"Beautiful, isn't it? You're right, by the way, Scent One, this is an Alaskan plant called Fireweed." She said kneeling to examine the dirt on the ground.

"Caroline, the white blooms are beautiful, the red is beautiful, and so, why are we playing in the dirt?" Rodger quipped.

"This is not dirt, it is soil." Caroline dusted her fingers and stood from her crouching position. "I don't know why I didn't notice it at first. All the soil in here has been shipped in. None of the soil, dirt as you call it, came from this island. Can you smell the difference?" Finally, Caroline turned to look at her husband.

"No, the only things I smell are flowers." Rodger didn't feel much like an investigator, but he had told the truth. He knew by the look in Caroline's eyes that they had best be finding an exit. They all but ran toward the door they used to come in.

Caroline slowed them down as she gazed at other plants.

They both froze in their tracks when they heard voices behind the door. Looking from one end to the other they realized, that that door was the only exit.

Rodger quickly scanned the nursery in hopes he had missed another way out. They had to hide. He tugged on Caroline's wrist and together they scooted to a table and crawled beneath it. Suddenly the flooring, 'soil' and all, began to shake and squeak.

They locked eyes with each other.

The floor began to sink like an elevator. Rodger squeezed his arms around Caroline and held her tight to his chest. The swishing sound was unheard by the two voices as they entered and shut the door behind them.

Down, down, they continued to float. A damp, large, dark room came into view, as their eyes adjusted. The perplexed couple stood and stepped off the brown, metal elevator. Once their weight freed their ride, it slowly began its ascension.

Caroline looked into the eyes of the investigator, knowing he was on the job. "Look who just showed up on my honeymoon; Detective Calvert." Caroline was grateful, especially as they both looked around in the earth-hewn tomb.

"Look Caroline, pipes are beaming light in from above." He pointed, but she did not move. "Caroline, are you okay?" Rodger's investigation turned to the concern on Caroline's face.

Her hand was covering her mouth. She whispered something Rodger could not unscramble. He turned back and eased next to her, not to startle her.

"What is that?" Rodger's eyes followed Caroline's gaze straight to a metal-plated circle at the center of the tomb's floor. Rodger took Caroline's hand and they walked, slowly, together, into earth-hewn belly.

Rodger stuttered slowly, "It, it, is a, a, a sundial."

"How is a sundial supposed to work underground?" Caroline questioned as she began looking around. She dug into her pouch wrapped around her waist. There she fumbled for her key ring. On it was a small light she often used when opening the car door, since she was careful not to scratch the paint around the keyhole. She shined it on the face of the sundial. "I suppose you could still tell time by it if you knew how to read the figures."

With those words, Rodger shot a concerned look at Caroline.

Again, they said it together, "W-e-i-r-d".

"This also could be dangerous. We need to find a way out of here," Rodger urged but Caroline became focused on the sundial's details.

Caroline bent from the waist, pinched, and then sniffed the dirt around the dial. "Island dirt," she showed the pinched dirt between her fingers to Rodger. Still in a bent position, she ran her fingers over the raised symbols along the outer edge. Caroline tried to sound out the gibberish and symbols around the sundial. Some appeared to be worn, cracked, Roman numerals.

"As in, look right now, Caroline." Rodger was looking for an exit. Glancing again at the sundial, he quickly identified dirty heel marks, possibly boots, clumped about the face of the symbols. Someone else had been here. He had no intention making their acquaintance, trapped, underground.

"Look for a way out. We know the way in. We can come back later." Rodger began pressing on the damp dirt walls as if a door would pop open. "Right now, we don't want to miss the lemonade and paddle boat ride." Rodger was trying to lighten the mood.

Caroline knew a secret door leading underground was not the ideal way to start learning about her inheritance. Nor did she intend spending their honeymoon in a damp, dirty hole in the ground.

Rodger reasoned that if someone caught them in their discovery they might be in danger. He suddenly recalled the Will's statement, "If you return."

Caroline looked at the ceiling where the metal elevator had quietly returned. It appeared to have lodged itself into a snug fit. It was Caroline, fighting the fear of having to walk amongst the spider webs, who decided to put her weight on the dirt floor where the elevator had dropped them off. With a swishing sound, dirt scattered into their eyes from above.

Rodger grabbed Caroline's forearm and slung her free of the descending metal ride. Once on the ground, they huddled into each other's arms, as before, and the ride returned them to the surface. Once again, they were beneath the table they had moved.

They carefully listened for voices or movement and heard only silence: an eerie silence.

Rodger whispered, "I think it is safe, Rosebud. Let's get out of here."

They quietly scrambled from beneath the table. Rodger's surveillance proved no nursery workers were around. No one! They bolted toward the door that had once been standing open, beckoning them inside. Now it was shut, but not for long. Caroline did not window-shop this time. Quickly, they made their escape and closed the door behind them.

Once outside, they both looked back toward Boldt Castle. Hand in hand, they strolled toward the gallant, rock-covered towers. Their hearts hadn't slowed to a normal pace when suddenly, reality slammed into them. They stood motionless. Before they started walking again, Caroline caught a glimmer through the azaleas off to her right. When her tennis shoes failed to move, Rodger turned to follow her scrutiny.

"Oh, no Rosebud," his lip quivered a little, "we've already fallen into one mystery, what are you gawking at now?" In his years of police service, Rodger had been shot at, nearly stabbed, been in more than a dozen high-speed auto chases, but this little gal could leave him shaking in his government issued steel-toed boots.

"Did you see something shiny out there?" His queen of mystery asked as she squeezed her eyes into one straight line.

"No," surely he said that too loud, "all I see is that paddle boat about to ride over to Fern Island. Don't you want to check out the sixty vessels and the captain's quarters?" Rodger nervously pointed toward the dock.

"I see something behind that gazebo. Let's go see what it is." He knew that was not a suggestion, she was already in motion. This bride was no rosebud, she was blossoming into trouble, and he knew it. Her instincts were as sharp as a military cadet in the Charleston, South Carolina academy, where he had trained.

They whizzed right by the gazebo. Odd. She especially loves gazebos. Rodger's parents were probably assembling the gazebo behind their duplex right now. They made Rodger promise not to tell Caroline about their gift to her garden. They wanted to be there when the couple returned so they could see the surprise on their new daughter-in-law's face. She wanted a gazebo so she could plant flowers around it and have a showcase for her hanging baskets.

So why were they dashing past this one?

Intuitive Women! Just last week one of the men had said every patrol car should have an intuitive woman as standard equipment. He must have been a married cop!

Now he finally understood the reality of it all. *They have instincts men don't. That marriage license would change him, all right.*

The paper Mr. Emanuel Bishop surprised them with, would have to stand in line.

Now, they were standing right in front of a huge bronze sundial. It was gorgeous! Symbols all over it, cryptic looking, like the one in the damp, dark tomb below the nursery. Raised numerals were glinting in the sunshine. Worn, unfamiliar etchings, somewhat like a time line or dispensational guide, captivated Rodger's attention.

"I've read that some families tell their generational stories through etchings. Some are carved into the very walls of their homes while others display their diaries in private gardens or cemeteries." Caroline hurried the history lesson while examining the face of the dial. "Rodger, look which way the dial is facing. Not toward the Seaway or the castle, but toward the nursery. Toward the other sundial."

Rodger walked around the sundial so he, too, would be facing the nursery. When he looked at the sundial, he realized she was right. The double digits were at the top. North.

The two sundials must be connected, but how?

For the first time since they set foot on Heart Island, Rodger became concerned for their safety. Caroline had already blundered her way into a mysterious hole in the ground, felt drawn to a sundial with strange symbols, but the oddest thing about it all was the fact she was the owner, the heir, of Boldt Castle.

Rodger had spotted the red eye of the video camera when they set foot on the dock. He thought it was just security for the Castle. He had not wanted to frighten Caroline, be he knew now, they were being followed.

Did someone know exactly who they were, and why they had mingled in with the tourist group?

Was he being an overprotective husband?

No!

It was not just habit.

Chapter 7

Rodger pointed toward the tourist group as they boarded the paddleboat. Rodger clasped Caroline's hand. Giggling and running, they ran past the tree stumps loaded with trays of lemonade and cookie crumbs. Cramming chunks of cookies into their mouths and jiggling cups of lemonade, they filed in line with the others.

"You two must be newlyweds," one of the older women at the back of line said with a raspy voice.

"Yes Ma'am, does it show that badly?" Rodger asked trying to whisper and act nonchalantly.

"Oh, yes dears. It shows." All three of the tourists shared a private giggle.

Rodger choked down the crispy sugar cookies and chased them down with the tart lemonade. His eyes were watering from the sting in the back of his throat. Caroline was waving her left hand over her mouth as if that would cool off the sudden tartness from her first gulp.

The little old lady turned and watched Caroline in amusement and asked, "Showing off that pretty, new ring, Mrs.?" Caroline coughed and sputtered into a laugh as they made their way onto the boat.

"Can we rent the Children's Play House?" Caroline's eyes were watching the island slip away as the paddleboat headed inland. She was imagining their next return to the island. With any luck at all Rodger would answer that question with a 'yes' and they would be packing their clothes and returning immediately. When Rodger did not answer, Caroline released her grip on the viewing rail and turned to see what must be holding him spellbound. Caroline glanced again as the island gradually faded into the distance. When her focus changed from the beauty of the coastline to inside the boat, she suddenly realized why she had not received an answer. No Rodger in sight. He was not standing right beside her, or behind her. After turning in every direction, Caroline's heart flooded with adrenaline. She was about to panic when she heard his voice calling her name.

"Caroline! Rosebud. I'm up here, at the helm," he shouted down to her seeing the fear wrinkling her brow. "I'm talking to the captain about a return visit. Come on up here. Take the steps just behind you."

Rodger's instructions were simple enough but suddenly she could not focus on the steps. The world got blurry and she could not feel her feet. She looked down at the first step, thinking the boat must be turning, making her dizzy. She felt a shove on her shoulder, which slightly turned her body to the right. Then the steps began to rise up to her and she saw a dark red glove passing her shoulder and jerking back again. The glove disappeared. The steps disappeared. Caroline felt pain on the left side of her face, then numbness, and the only thing she could hear was her own breathing.

It took a few minutes before anyone noticed Caroline had collapsed on the bottom steps of the paddleboat. A man, who had been standing beside Caroline at the rail, was the first to reach her crumpled body.

Rodger realized she had not scaled the steps.

What was taking her so long?

Before Rodger could take two steps backwards and look down the stairway, a woman screamed. When Rodger caught sight of the top of Caroline's parted hair and pigtails, he stumbled with each galloping step. He felt his heart stop when he reached her.

She was unconscious.

Limp, but breathing.

The detective kicked in as soon as the husband slowed his brain from a panic attack. Instincts from training clocked in as he surveyed faces standing nearby. Rodger quickly pulled Caroline onto his lap and bent Caroline's head between her knees. He could not remember if she had finished her cookies or not, so he pulled both arms into her abdomen and lifted her three times, performing the Heimlich maneuver, hoping to clear her breathing passageway. Nothing he did revived her. He felt her slowing pulse as more and more faces gathered around them.

Someone yelled up to the captain to call ahead and order an ambulance to transport one of the passengers.

The paddleboat gained speed and soon they reached the New York shore. As the crowd separated, three men dressed in white uniforms carrying a stretcher came into Rodger's view.

In moments, one of the men lifted Caroline from Rodger's embrace. The men seemed to struggle with awkwardness as they finagled Caroline's limbs onto their stretcher. When the man in front lifted his poles, Rodger stepped in behind him so he could be close to Caroline's face, just in case she woke up and was startled.

It took the rescue crew several moments to secure Caroline inside the ambulance. They had insisted Rodger wait outside because there was not enough room to work with a third person in the tight quarters. One man was kneeling to the right of Caroline when suddenly gravel was flung onto Rodger's legs as the van bolted away, allowing the double doors to slam on their own.

In shock, Rodger began running after the ambulance. He had dashed about three yards when he heard a siren. Rodger stopped in his tracks. His hands became cold as ice. He watched Caroline's van racing away.

A second ambulance pulled up to the dock. They were answering the boat captain's call.

Without a word, Rodger fled to his rental car and followed his bride. Cell phone in hand, Rodger called his office. He punched in the private desk code on the keypad and reached a gruff voice.

"What?"

Without a greeting Rodger demanded, "Nathan, run this tag. I need an address. Now!"

From the familiar strain in his voice, Nathan knew Rodger had to be in pursuit of something. He did not ask, knowing the investigator was supposed to be on his honeymoon.

"No cracks, this is an emergency."

"Yes sir. Street address is 610 Converse Street, New York. Give me your location and I'll get you there", Nathan was quick, professional and had a natural nose for when to kid around and when to kick into action. He was in kick mode. He provided every turn, including landmarks. He asked Rodger what he was driving and Nathan picked him up on satellite. "What are we chasing, Rodger?" Nathan waited for his response as he focused on moving satellite images.

"A white commercial van", Rodger was straight to the point.

"It just turned left in front of you into a warehouse with a flat top. Should be in your sight in 4-3-2-1; turn left now. STOP, Rodger! Do not go in there. Wait." Nathan held his breath.

Rodger trusted his fellow officer's instincts. Therefore, he waited. He waited. He waited.

"Rodger, a van just exited the opposite side of that building. Wait Rodger! Do not move yet. No. That cannot be the same van. Exhaust is different", Nathan's observation sent Rodger's eyebrows upward in amazement. Not only could he breach privacy but also he actually noticed such a minute detail like exhaust fumes. "I infrared scanned the van as you chased it into the building. Four bodies were inside. The van exiting the other side has only three occupants. Are you going inside the building, officer Rodger?" Nathan waited on his reply.

"I'm going in! Send me silent back-up, just in case. Can you see an entrance from the roof?" Rodger asked, as he was already halfway up the ladder mounted to the exterior.

"Yes. I see you now, on the north side. Go to the opposite side, south center. There appears to be a skylight. It should open. I also see a hidden dish, so I hope they do not see us looking at them. Go behind it. It is the little mound to your left about three feet from the edge of the roof. If it doesn't move, it doesn't have sensory scan", Nathan let out a puff of air. He watched as Rodger's tiny speck moved across the screen.

"I'm moving undetected, Nathan. Is that good?"

"No. That means your van is not CIA nor could it be FBI. You are dealing with bad boys. Be careful. You got a weapon?" Nathan knew the answer. His gut tightened.

"Me? Without my 'piece' of mind? Never! Of course I have my weapon." Rodger listened as Nathan squeezed out the breath he had been holding.

The skylight was too dingy to see through. Rodger eased the top aside. The element of surprise was the game plan. With the cell phone turned to silent mode, Rodger began the descent into the warehouse. He did not hear voices. He smelled a cigar, no cigarettes. Nothing else was recognizable from that height.

He was crawling on the catwalk when he heard a moan.

He froze.

Looking in every direction, he waited for another sound to reach his ears. He hoped the sound would be louder than the fast-paced heartbeats pounding against his eardrums. Then he heard it again. He crawled about three more feet and bit his lower lip to stifle a gasp when he caught a quick glimpse of pigtails frantically swishing around on the cot just inside the double doors of the van. After looking in every direction possible, without exposing his position, Rodger began to inch his way down the ladder. He looked for explosives around the white rescue van they had used to kidnap Caroline.

When Rodger reached the grimy concrete floor, he made his way quickly to Caroline and saw that she was conscious. He laid his finger to his lips to tell her not to make a sound as he untied her hands, feet, and removed the duct tape from her mouth. She shook her head; her eyes looked wobbly to Rodger. He instantly knew someone drugged his wife. The investigative husband was watchful while he untied his bride and looked for a needle mark at the same time.

Once freed, she gasped for air.

Rodger had to grab her to keep her from standing on her own. She wanted out of the van.

The look in her eyes told him she was unstable, and he should not allow her to walk on her own. Something else in her eyes told him she would try.

"Ugh, R-o-d-g-e-r, where am I? W-h-a-t is this plaaace?" Caroline was frightened to tears but wanted answers before she fell apart.

"My mouth is so dry. The room is spinning. Slow-l-y spinning. I think I'm going to", she did.

Rodger held her at the waist and pushed her face forward away from his shoes.

"You'll be okay in a minute, Rosebud." Rodger tried to comfort her. He held her forehead and encouraged her to empty her stomach.

She had no idea drugs had mingled with cookies and lemonade.

Rodger knew. He found the tiny pin mark on the back of Caroline's neck and rubbed it lightly so the rest of the drug would leave her body quickly. Gently rubbing the red pinpricked area, he tried to smell the liquid.

"If I had my suitcase, I could find out what drug they used." Rodger grunted to himself.

"Okay, where are we?" Caroline demanded.

She was confused but adamant while wiping her mouth with the bottom of her shirt.

"I think we need to move. I will tell you when we get to the rental car. Put your arm around my neck and I'll guide you with my arm around your waist." Rodger instructed Caroline of his every move. She was weaving and still dizzy but they needed to get out of that building. Rodger walked Caroline, more like waltzed with her, to the door from which the van had entered. Together they pushed the door open. When the light from outside hit Caroline's blurred vision, she doubled over, miraculously missing Rodger's shoes, again.

Chapter 8

Feeling safe in the hotel room, Rodger slumped into a large chair near the sliding glass doors. Caroline was resting on the bed, probably dozing again. Rodger started to open the curtains to the sliding glass doors when he spotted an odd color shining through. He pulled the curtains apart. Across both doors, someone used paint to leave them a threatening message.

"Leave now. Don't come here again or next time you will be pushing up daisies!"

Rodger grabbed his camera and made digital pictures of both the inside and the outside of the doors. He made pictures and took samples of the ground on the outside. Using paper towels from the kitchenette, he gathered dirt, dead bugs, and rocks, for possible evidence. Then he washed the paint with his shampoo. He took the yellow paint stained towels and dumped them on the second shelf of a maid's cart, just outside their door. He would not let Caroline see the threat.

The letters, written on the outside, he read perfectly from the inside. The writer had to reverse the letters, like using a mirror. That takes time and Rodger had a good idea just how much time it might have taken.

The newlyweds called for room service to deliver their dinner. Still weak and shaken, Caroline decided to model her new purchases she had chosen from a nearby dress shop. Rodger's eyes darted back and forth, swiping away the pictures in both of their minds, clearing out the day's events. Feeling more relaxed, they settled in for a movie, a taste of wine, and romance. Rodger knew they could not 'hold up' in their honeymoon motel. He was surprised to feel the newness of emotions charging through him. He was protector, provider, lover, and even entertainer.

He was a husband.

The night was slipping away. Rodger would be the first to awaken and see the morning light peeping through the clean sliding glass doors.

"Let it be a safe, beautiful day, Lord, and please give me some answers," Rodger whispered his prayer just as Caroline opened her eyes and stretched up to kiss her husband on his prayerful lips.

Secretly, Caroline had waited until she was sure he had finished his prayer.

After breakfast in bed, they got their 'brave' on, as Caroline put it, and headed for the library. They decided they needed more history and information about Heart Island before they returned for another tour. Rodger knew that would give him enough time to email his office the details of what had happened and be able to leave the evidence in a safe place for pick-up.

Caroline was packed and ready to face, whatever. "Scent One," Caroline began, in her brave voice, as they rode the elevator down to the parking garage, "I hope you realize that the Devil only attacks what he fears. So, if he is afraid of us owning Heart Island, then what am I supposed to do with it?"

Rodger thought for a moment too long and replied, "Good question. I was hoping for more answers but somehow you have managed to find more questions. The other detectives said I would be a better agent when I became a husband. I'm beginning to understand."

Giggling, they put their luggage in the trunk of the new rental and used the GPS to locate the library. Hopefully, they would find some answers there. That is all, just answers.

There was no shortage of books, maps, and photos of Heart Island. The story was a sad one. George's wife never lived in the gift her husband built for her and their two daughters. When she passed away, George halted the builder's work teams, and he never returned to the castle. Rodger glanced at Caroline, her hair draping over one eye as she studied a book opened on the table and wondered if she would fulfill George's dreams and live on the island.

Was someone trying to stop that from happening? One answer came to Rodger. A Bible Queen, Esther, believed her life was a piece to a puzzle when she said she was alive for that day, "For such a time as this". This is why he became a detective. Every piece to the puzzle had its place. He needed the dry erase board at work so he could visually organize all the facts. He needed the expert team members at his office.

One new question was on both of their minds. Should they return to Heart Island?

Caroline tossed her hair over one shoulder, and said, "Scent One, we better get moving. You can't smell a single flower from Heart Island here." Her smile, although mischievous, answered the question.

"Rosebud, let's get dressed. We have another tour to take," Rodger said as he pulled on his tennis shoes.

Caroline slammed the book closed and dashed to get dressed. She reached inside her carryon and found a book labeled "Horticulturists Are Handy". She opened it to show a hole dug out in the center of the book. Inside the hole were two rusty keys on a key ring, a butterfly locket, and a large rusty skeleton key with a sundial emblem on its top.

"Good hiding place, don't you think, Mr. Spy? My mom never found this secret stash." Caroline's beaming smile went from victory to forlorn, "Then again, she isn't really my mom. This whole inherited island and castle thing has thrown my mind into an exasperating void."

Before Caroline could finish, Rodger said, "Caroline, you always use 'exasperated' when you don't know what is going on."

"It is as if I don't know who I am. I am a new wife with a very interesting background. I thought I was just an adopted girl from nowhere. Now it seems I was royalty at some point in time. Why was I put up for adoption if my family owned an island with a castle on it? Someone loved plants like I do. Someone gave me away. How could they have abandoned their child?" Caroline rambled.

Rodger crossed the distance between them with his arms held out wide. He knew she was going to cry. As he held her, she lifted her head from his chest and looked into his eyes.

"I don't always use 'exasperated'", Caroline whined.

"Yes, you do. Next time I'll point it out to you. Deal?" They snickered as they held each other. "Good job hiding the keys and locket. I might have an opening at the 'spy job' as you call it. If you are ready, let me hide the keys on me and we can be off on our adventure."

Before Rodger could say another word, Caroline confirmed with closure, "Deal!"

Rodger hid the three keys inside his left boot that usually concealed a Derringer. The weapon went into his jeans pocket along with his badge.

Caroline was observing the details and asked, "Rodger, should I take the locket or leave it in the book?" Instinct began kicking in. Instinct you don't get with experience. Rodger took the locket and gently unfastened the old brackets. Caroline gathered her hair and lifted it so her husband could fasten the slightly tarnished silver chain around her neck. He did so and began to snuggle into her scented hair, neck, and ear.

Caroline responded, nuzzling his gentleness but pulled away saying, "Mr. Spy, partner, we won't get any work done if we stay here".

They both laughed and started for the door. Rodger gently placed his hand on the small of her back, realizing he was her husband, partner in an investigation, but right now, he was her protector.

Chapter 9

The ride to the Island was beautiful and flawless. Rodger noticed one of his detectives from the office standing at the back of the paddleboat. He was one of Nathan's men. One finger was pointing to a small piece of cloth hanging out of his pocket with a dab of yellow coloring smeared on it. When he knew Rodger had seen it, he tossed it overboard with a move resembling a magician's sleight of hand. Rodger's confidence in his backup team put him more at ease. His eyes were not the only ones protecting his wife.

The men would not make eye contact the rest of the day.

Rodger knew his phone call to the lab geeks would not only send someone for the package he bundled and left in the parking garage, but would also alert the detectives that he and Caroline were in danger.

Good guys, better partners. Rodger always knew they would stick together.

Rodger knew the detective was arranging a meeting, so they could trade information. His staff would secure the area. Rodger had only to wait for the carefully planned opportunity. Right now, he had to decide where Caroline and those keys needed to be, in broad daylight.

The boat docked and the tour began. Caroline nudged Rodger off behind a gardenia bush and kissed him.

"Covert maneuvers. How do you like my plan so far?"

They kissed again.

"I love your plan, Rosebud; now what?" Rodger kissed her so hard she blushed.

"Wow, you made the bride blush right behind the gardenias, Scent One. Or should we have secret agent names?" Caroline was so serious Rodger could not help but laugh at her.

"If you give me a flower name, I'll leave you on this island." They both giggled and held hands as they walked toward the garden. Their instincts, together, were better than Rodger's team. Without discussing directions or plans, their feet headed for the greenhouse.

"Unison, that is what they call it. Unison." Rodger studied their feet, as they seemed to be in a perfectly choreographed march. They arrived at the greenhouse and found the door ajar. They looked in every direction and then peeked inside. No one was there. They moved the door about two inches and listened for voices or noise. The quiet was eerie. They slid past the slightly opened door and stopped just inside to look around. They walked toward the area where they had crouched the day before. Now the area looked neatly swept. They moved a clay pot, lifted the hatch covered with fine dirt and they bounded, one at a time, into the dark womb that opened with the familiar swishing sound beneath their feet.

"It is damper than I remember." Caroline said rubbing her arms from the slight chill.

"There it is Rosebud, the sundial." Rodger reached in his boot to uncover the two rings on the key ring.

"Wait, Rodger," Caroline said grasping his forearm. The sundial is on the largest of the three keys. It is the one by itself, not on the key ring." Caroline's eyes were big as saucers as she stared at the sundial on the ground. Rodger adjusted the flooring above their heads into a tight fit, and then bent to examine the sundial. Neither of them could find a hole where the key would fit. The damp earth revealed large sized footprints all around the sundial, even more than there were two days ago. Rodger knelt with one knee on the complex design and held the key in front for both of them to examine. Caroline shined her small key ring light on the areas Rodger was sweeping with his hands. They looked at the words written around the outside of the damp metal sundial. Rodger began leaning over to get a better look at the writing. He did not recognize any of the symbols.

When both hands were planted on the dial, he and Caroline began to read aloud, in unison. ***"Today is yesterday, without fear. Dial tomorrow while it is near. Lock yourself inside before the three collide. Salvage life in the bud before the darkening of the Scud."***

Rodger bolted up from the ground nearly knocking Caroline backwards. They looked at each other but did not dare say 'weird'.

"We couldn't read a word on that sundial. When I put both hands on its face, we could both read the symbols . . . well; they were in English, weren't they?" Rodger asked as he swiped at his beads of sweat gathering on his forehead. Caroline was sweating, too.

"I can't read the symbols right now. Can you?" She asked, shining the small light onto the sundial's face.

"No." Rodger said, not bothering to wipe the sweat rolling over his eyelids. "I am going to bend down, and place my hands on the sundial again; don't touch me this time, and try reading the words aloud, if you can." Rodger said as he gave Caroline the instructions he was not quite wrapping his own mind around.

Rodger knelt, placed both hands on the sundial, and read the first three words. Caroline was amazed that she could not read a word nor recognize a symbol. She placed her hand on Rodger's back where it had been last time he had knelt there. She instantly read the first sentence. She removed her hand from Rodger's back and the illegible symbols reappeared.

"This is too weird, Rodger. I do not understand what is happening! This is exasperating", Caroline threw both hands up into the air as she watched Rodger stand to his feet.

"You did it, again." He explained.

"I did what again?"

He recognized the challenged look on her face when she used the word 'exasperated'. Rodger decided to let it go. "Rosebud, why don't we read the words together, after I put my hands on the dial and you put your hands on my back. Okay?" Rodger's words were sharp enough to cut through tin.

"Okay. Let's do it."

Rodger knelt again, placed both hands on the sundial, and waited for Caroline to put her hands on his back. After a moment of hesitation, she followed through with their plan. Their voices, each distinct, bounced off the walls of the underground room as they spoke the words, aloud.

"Together now . . . one, two, three . . . *'Today is yesterday without fear. Dial tomorrow while it is near. Lock yourself inside before the three collide. Salvage life in the bud before . . . the darkening of the Scud'*."

The room became transparent. Blue rivers resembling water began to swirl around them. The blue was more like wind rather than tangible liquid.

Caroline removed her hand from Rodger's back. The sundial seemed to tilt slightly and come to rest with a loud jarring thud. The blue changed to a turquoise color, illuminating the face of the sundial. The triangular sun-caster sitting up made a high-pitched sound and one end jetted into the air. Underneath there was a deep crevice. Rodger looked inside and glanced at the large key with a sundial as its top handle.

Caroline saw it at the same time and said, "Quick, Rodger, 'lock yourself inside before the three collide', put the big key in the hole, sideways." Caroline pointed, "Right there, under the caster, in the grooved opening".

Rodger placed the big rusty key into the slot. It was a perfect fit. The key snapped into place, causing the transparent blue and turquoise waves of light to stop so suddenly, the air remained charged with dazzling anticipation.

Chapter 10

They were above ground. The sudden brightness of the sun cleared the dizziness from their eyes but it did not clarify the answer as to how they got outside. Rodger stood and fixed his eyes on Caroline. "How did you know to do that?" Caroline stepped back and took a deep breath. It was a shaky breath. "Are you all right, darling?" Rodger braced her by holding her arms to steady her footing. She was shaken, but very alert.

After looking around at the unfamiliar territory, Rodger whispered, "I think this is out of my jurisdiction."

Caroline could not believe her eyes. The evergreens and plants were huge.

Rodger looked down at the sundial. "Did the sundial decipher that we spoke English? How did we understand the letters unless it changed them so we could read the words? Caroline, do you think it changed our understanding or the actual letters?" Rodger had asked three questions of two deaf ears.

Caroline was wandering around looking at the foliage. In amazement, she stood holding leaves that she had only read about in horticultural history books. These plants had been extinct for decades, and longer.

Rodger was surveying the area but his eyes were on Caroline as she scratched at the textures of different leaves. She was snapping stems in half and was sniffing them when Rodger asked, "If we are outside now, where is the greenhouse?"

Caroline began running first. Rodger followed in quick pursuit. The greenhouse was right where it always had been. The underground sundial had led them to the garden where they had visited another sundial earlier that day.

Panting for breath Rodger said, "Caroline do you realize we started out under the greenhouse and ended up in the middle of the island, above ground, at a different sundial?"

"Yes, officer, I do. That is why I am running to see if there is a greenhouse and if there is a sundial underground." The greenhouse came into view. The upkeep of the unit was incredible. High-tech comes to mind. They were not surprised to find the door locked.

Rodger lifted the second key they had received from his pocket. It was a perfect fit. The door opened with an airtight swishing sound. It slid open to the right, disappearing into the wall. They cautiously stepped inside. The door swooshed closed behind them. Lights automatically came on, along the floor and in the ceiling.

The atmosphere changed.

They stopped, frozen in their paths, looked around in disbelief and then at each other.

"Caroline, I am not great with plants, but I know enough to confidently say I've never seen anything like this in my entire life. What is this?"

It took Caroline a moment to answer.

"I believe we are looking at the future of greenhouses. What I cannot understand is how extinct plants are thriving, here, in the future. This must be the future! How is it possible *we* are here in the future?"

Then Caroline was at a total loss of words.

Rodger saw a beautiful red plant just off to their right. To take a closer look he pushed aside a branch of an unfamiliar root-bound shrub in a larger-than-life sized bucket. He was about to gather the reddish bloom into his palm when he heard a shrill cry.

"NO! Rodger, don't touch that bloom!"

Caroline had shouted with such a high-pitched tone that it made them both shutter.

"Rodger, it is a Labrador Tea plant. Extinct so many years ago that only horticulturists would have any idea what it was, ugh, is. It was used for arthritis, but it can make you very dizzy just by touching the leaves." Caroline had made her way over to the plant to examine its beautiful foliage. Glancing upward, Caroline studied the reddish-brown blooms, as they loomed overhead. "Scent One, take a sniff of this boom, but be careful not to touch the white fuzzy seeds on the top. Alaskans named this plant Fireweed because of its reddish stalks."

Rodger and Caroline put their arms around each other, as their eyes roamed in every direction. Extinct plants filled the room. Caroline examined several large glass beakers, each carefully filled with plant tissue cultures. There were a few variations, but Orchids out-numbered everything.

"Orchids? What properties would someone look for in orchids?" Caroline questioned.

Rodger looked through the beaker in Caroline's tight, trembling fingers and asked, "Are those orchids extinct, too?"

Caroline nodded a feeble 'yes' as she carefully replaced someone's research.

"What if we are not in the future? You said everything we see is extinct. What if we are somehow in the past?" No sooner than the words had come out of his mouth, Rodger threw his hands up in the air and gave a disgusted grunt. "Ugh! Listen to me. I have gone crazy. Past, future, what am I saying?"

Caroline swung around in front of her husband to face him and the reality of their situation. "I have an idea. Let's find out which it is. The sundial obviously has changed time and taken us with it. If we go to the mansion, we will find out exactly what year it is, or at least what stage of construction has been completed. We read the history on the mansion and we saw the photos of the building projects marked by decades. I hate to leave without seeing more of this greenhouse but I think right now we need some answers." Caroline was already tugging her husband out the door as he removed the key from his pocket. Once outside Rodger securely locked the sliding door and they quickly made their way toward the mansion.

Caroline was two steps ahead of Rodger, and he was checking out perimeters, as usual. As they approached the mansion, they saw men dressed in brilliant blue and purple trimmed overalls.

Their work suits looked almost metallic in color. The men picked up lumber and what looked like buckets of nails. They were working on a new addition to the mansion. They couldn't see anything new attached to the structure on the outside so they began moving to their right.

"Okay, the mansion looks the same, so where is the construction site? Caroline, stay close to me, and we will circle the mansion. Keep a keen eye out for anything that looks different from our tour. I will be watching for people, security, and the blue space suit team." Rodger hoped she heard what he said; his focus was on keeping them safe.

They crept around shrubs, roses, trees, and anything that would camouflage their undercover work. They managed to make their way, undetected, all the way around the mansion. No one was near the dock or the playhouse. When they stopped behind an azalea, where they had begun their search, they dropped down to their knees.

"Now what? Nothing. Not one change. So, where is the new construction?"

Caroline was . . .

"I'm exasperated, and totally confused. You aren't disappointed in my detective skills, are you? Are you Rodger?" Caroline turned to see the expression on his face looking just like she felt.

"Once again," Rodger, ignoring her question, moved on, "we have more questions than answers. Of course, you know this means we have to get inside the mansion. We need to see the hall of pictures to get an idea of what is going on here."

The white in Caroline's widening eyes was bright enough to illuminate the darkness. Rodger could not help but snicker at her.

"Don't give me that look. I know you. I know exactly what you are thinking. We haven't been married a week yet, and I already am acting like a well-trained husband."

Caroline bent her face to her knees and slapped her fingers over her mouth to snicker.

"Yes, Scent One, but you can never say this marriage is dull or unexciting." Caroline made them both laugh with that description.

Rodger, still squatting in front of Caroline, took her by the shoulders and said, "Seems to me that if you inherited this mansion and island then it should belong to you in the future as well".

Caroline stood to her feet. "Yeah, you are right!"

"So it won't hurt a thing for the owners to visit their mansion, now will it?" Rodger asked as he stood up.

"You cannot trespass on your own property. Let's go!" Caroline winked at her cop.

Like the understanding husband he had become, they held hands and silently made their way to the back entrance.

Chapter 11

The back door had a digital keypad lock. Caroline saw the uneasiness on Rodger's face and asked, "We only have three tries, right?" Rodger never offered to try to guess, he just moved aside and let her take the first try. Caroline put her fingers over the keyboard. Her fingers dangled in midair like frozen icicles, awaiting a brilliant idea. Caroline typed in her birth date.

Both of them holding their breath stiffened at the inactivity of the lighted pad. With a whooshing sound, first from the door, and second from each of them, they scurried inside the door.

"That was too easy." Rodger realized his words had come out of his mouth without thinking about their impact. For the first time, Caroline stopped in her tracks while Rodger forged ahead. He stopped, looked over his right shoulder, and asked, "Caroline, are you all right?" She squeezed out the answer like toothpaste from its tube.

"NnnnOooo, I am afraid. I really am afraid. What is going on here? Rodger, someone knew my exact birth date. That someone obviously lives here, in the future."

Rodger glanced back to see Caroline standing just inside the doorframe, and saw her rigid arms and two balled up fists.

"Rosebud, you might have been the one who built the greenhouse, and set the combination on that lock. We will not know until we investigate further. There is no one to call for help. We have to do this, alone, now. Take my hand, and let's go inside and try to figure this out. I love you. I am just as afraid and confused as you are. Whatever we find, we find it together."

Caroline's trembling lips failed to answer, but her heart trusted in Rodger's ability to take care of both of them. She nodded her head, gripped his hand, and silently they continued inside the mansion.

The investigator mode kicked in. Rodger said, "Keep your eyes open. If you see anything or anybody, squeeze my hand but do not say a word. If I stop, you look behind us. I will be looking ahead. Do you understand, Caroline?"

Instead of answering, she squeezed his hand.

She noticed he called her Caroline instead of Rosebud.

"Good, we can do this together. Let's check out the kitchen first." Rodger glanced at her soft trusting hand inside of his. Determined he would never let her down, Rodger, grateful for his unwavering faith, cried out to the Lord.

They made their way through the corridors where staff stored their lodgings. The silver swinging double doors glided open easily. The kitchen smelled sweet, like warm cake. One automatic dishwasher, out of three, was still humming, completing its drying cycle.

"Dessert must have been good. The smell is still lingering," Rodger said as he was sniffing the air. He listened but heard no voices.

They made their way along the left wall where built-in cabinets stood ten feet high. A chopping board, island table, would hide them if anyone entered the room from any of the three doors. They pushed through one set of doors into the dining room. The table seated twenty. The red mahogany was rich against the fabric inlays on the walls. It smelled of the comfort that comes when you encounter heavy wood. Inviting. Sturdy. Empty, however, it was overwhelming.

"If dinner was served in here, the aroma of it is gone. Keep sniffing and see if we can detect that sweet scent we found in the kitchen. If we do, we might find the dinner guests, or at least, whoever set the dishwasher's timer." Rodger did not wait for an answer, but kept up their slow pace, holding on tight to Caroline's hand.

They exited the dining room and inched their way between the two sitting parlors. The men's had the odor of pipes and cigarettes.

The beautifully arranged gardenias atop the fireplace mantel filled the feminine parlor with a relaxing, welcoming scent.

Vacant.

No voices.

No one was to enjoy the lovely rooms.

"Nobody," Caroline whispered into Rodger's ear.

"No kidding," he quickly whispered his response.

As they continued in the hallway toward the entertainment rooms, Caroline froze in her tracks, making Rodger stumble forward. She squeezed his fingers.

He turned to see which direction she was looking and why she had stopped. Her eyes strained at the wall to their left. Rodger let go of her hand, turned, his pose mimicking Caroline's frozen stance.

The photo was of the two of them. They were older. They were sitting on the front steps of the mansion. Four children sat at their feet. Two of the children were dressed exactly alike and had identical facial and physical features.

"Twins." That was all Caroline said, in a wispy voice that lifted the air, just before she fainted.

Rodger lunged backward to grab Caroline as she crumpled at his feet. They tumbled together onto the lush hallway carpet. He leaned her back against the wall and shoved her head between her knees.

He hated to leave her but he ran to the kitchen. Quickly finding a glass he got enough water to splash on her face and provide her with a few sips. He jostled the glass of water in his uneven dash to reach her side.

It was a good thing most of the water was gone.

He dropped the glass on the carpet when he realized she was gone.

Everything in his mind began to tumble and jumble together like pick-up-sticks. Nothing was making sense. On every turn, someone was trying to separate him from Caroline.

Why had he left her in that hall? He was beating himself up pretty bad when he noticed the impression left on the freshly vacuumed carpet.

He followed Caroline's heel marks into the library. Her rutted impressions stopped in front of one of the many bookcases built into the room's wall.

"It was the husband who left her out there in the hall, now let's see if the officer can find her", Rodger was being harder on himself than Caroline would, if he ever found her.

Straddling the last two indentions where her heel marks trailed off into thin air, he noticed a shuffled amount of carpet to one side of the bookshelf. Frantic, Rodger began pushing and pulling on everything sitting and attached, flower vase, books, carved wooden overlays, nothing happened. Frustrated, Rodger took several deep breaths and let each one out slowly. A large leather-bound book on the top shelf caught Rodger's attention.

The book's title, burned into the wine-colored leather binder read, "*The Sundial*".

Raising a trembling arm, Rodger gently touched the binder of the book. Nothing happened. Then he pushed the book.

Nothing.

Grinding his teeth, he grabbed the book into his suddenly steady palm and clinched each fingertip with force enough to turn them white, and pulled. The frame of the bookcase gave a jolt, squeaked, and began moving inward. Rodger sucked in half of the library's air into his lungs and blew it out again. He flattened himself against the adjoining bookshelf, and slid into another room.

The air was thick with musty dampness. Crumpled at his feet, slumped against the wall, was Caroline.

Stooping to revive the love of his life, he noted the freshly pounded-in dusty tracks. The officer made a mental note to figure out what drags women, has no feet, but moves on a track, of sorts.

Chapter 12

Lifting Caroline into his arms, he considered the trail he would follow, later. Right now, he had to revive and protect his wife. Turning with Caroline in his arms, Rodger watched the wall of the bookcase tightly close and lock into place. He sat down, nesting Caroline's limp body into his lap.

Before he could look for needle marks on her arms or a bleeding gash on the back of her head, she stirred, moaned, and opened her glassy eyes. She was about to scream as she noticed her surroundings but Rodger gently placed his hand over her mouth. She refrained herself as she looked around at the wood-studded framework and then at the narrow corridor.

"Where are we? Why did you bring me in here?" Caroline asked in a whisper. Her eyes were huge, and her eyebrows had grown into a straight line.

"Caroline. Rosebud", Rodger prepared to answer her as he wiped her damp forehead with his fingertips, "I did not bring you here. Someone drug you here. We are behind a bookcase in the library."

Caroline sat straight up, pursed her lips to speak, but fainted, again.

Rodger was so relieved he was holding Caroline and they were safe he whispered into her hair, "I never knew I had this effect on women. What happens in the office stays in the office, or, ugh, the hidden wall space." Rodger's chest rose and fell with a snicker. It seemed to lighten his burden, or at least help him clear his mind. Then he realized the cramped space and limber bride was putting a strain on his folded legs.

Seven minutes later, when Caroline was fully alert, they stood and faced the concrete block walls that led to a winding corridor. It was wide enough for only one person at a time. Rodger stepped into the narrow tunnel-like walkway, and Caroline gripped the back of his belt buckle. After what seemed like a lifetime, or about fifty steps, they agreed they were descending. The damp coolness was enough proof.

A greenish light appeared to be ahead of them, rounding the corner, they had no idea what to expect. The descending walkway emptied into a large basement.

"Underground, again". Rodger whispered. They stood side by side in a basement with a well-lighted green house. There were no windows, just artificial lighting. At the center of the room was a metallic gazebo, enclosed in glass. Plants were everywhere. Beakers, filled to overflowing, lined a counter top.

It was like being in a jungle with glass, wood, and no sunshine.

Tables were organized and labeled with tropical plants. One table held several computers, which were lit up with research information.

Rodger pulling Caroline in front of him, massaged her shoulders, and asked, "Where do you want to start this time?"

Without flinching, she said, "The gazebo".

Rodger gripped her shoulders tightly, still planning their next move, "Okay, but this time, we stick together."

Trotting in sync, they gave passing glances at the computer screens and extinct plants.

The beauty surrounding her felt like a dream.

Half expecting the floor to creak beneath them, together they slowly moved forward. Making sure they 'stuck together' Rodger grasped Caroline's fidgety fingers into his reassuring grip.

Caroline's eyes were on the gazebo.

Rodger's eyes scanned the room like a cop.

Caroline cautiously reached out and touched the gazebo.

Rodger squeezed her hand. "Thanks for the reassurance", she said looking at their fists intertwined.

Rodger nodded, and smiled with the knowledge that his reassurance was loaded and strapped to his ankle.

Working together, neither hesitated to step inside the gazebo. In the center was a gleaming silver sundial.

Side by side, they took baby steps. A series of lights, just above their heads, began to flash. The thick tube-shaped lights were greenish-purple and similar to florescent lighting. Warmth began to radiate from the lighting and computer-like sounds began to chatter with unfamiliar tones. One almost sounded like a baby cat crying. Another sounded like a flute in distress. Together they stepped out of the gazebo and the lights changed to brilliant blue and then suddenly, motionless.

"Did we interrupt some kind of sequence?" Caroline asked grasping for a piece to the newest puzzle. Before either could make another guess, a computer voice made a loud request.

"Welcome Master Rodger, what is your voice action command?" Then silence.

"How do you know I am Rodger?" He asked the computer.

"Your weight is reduced but your voice matches purification sound wave analysis. I scanned your retina before sounding the alarm to destruct. Next VAC, Sir Calvert", the computer answered and was ready to move on.

Sir Calvert was not ready to move.

Caroline estimated that curiosity was all that was between him and fainting.

Rodger asked the computer, "What is VAC?"

Without hesitation, the computer replied, "VAC is your program, Sir Calvert; it is an acronym for Voice Action Command."

Rodger looked in every direction and then asked, "What is your name?" The computer responded, "You named me Rosebudial, Sir."

Caroline turned to face Rodger. Caroline's mouth instantly went dry, making her words squeaky, "We are standing in an underground gazebo, and you are talking to a computer".

Rodger was almost nose to nose with Caroline when he said, "The computer is answering back. And you look pale in this purple lighting."

"Rodger, I will never faint again because I am afraid I will miss something." She held his attention in a fierce grip. "Rodger. Rodger, you are having a conversation with a computer. I suggest we step away from this gazebo and ask a few more questions", Caroline began stepping further away, almost dragging Rodger, as she made her plea.

Without another word, they stepped several feet away from the gazebo. Rosebudial made a swirling sound that startled them both but ended quickly with the greenish-purple lights fading.

"Sir, you have a potential misfire in chamber three. I suggest you disengage said bullet from your revolver."

Rodger's eyes veered to Caroline.

Her raised brow said it all. "You are packing?" Rodger knelt, pulled up his pants leg, and retrieved the small handgun. He spun the chamber and pulled out bullet number three. He reached into the small pouch attached to the belt around his calf and pulled out a replacement. He was ready to reload the empty chamber when the computer startled him.

"Sir, that bullet also has a flaw. Do you wish me to scan for fingerprints and DNA?"

Rodger stammered, "Nnuuno. Yes! What would you have me do with these two bullets?" He thought that was a good question.

Rosebudial paused a bit too long before replying, "Completed task. Caszone."

Rodger and Caroline locked eyes with one another. Rodger's eyes were searching Caroline's to see if there was any recognition of a family member.

Caroline's eyes were waiting for Rodger's explanation for playing cop on their honeymoon.

In perfect unison they asked, "Who is Caszone?"

Rodger broke the stare-down and twisted his head in every direction, not sure, where the face of the computer might be.

"Sir, please place the bullets on the center of the silver work table to your right and step away."

Rodger moved to the opposite side of the room and placed the two bullets on what looked like a silver polished dinner plate, in the center of the table. As he backed away, Caroline's hand was reaching for the crook of his arm.

"Further away, Sir." Rosebudial instructed.

They moved back six more steps. Thick clear sheeting fell from the ceiling separating them from the rest of the room. It looked like a cocoon. A clear tube descended from the ceiling, sealing the plate and the two bullets in a vacuum tight cylinder. First, there was a sucking sound and the bullets did not move. Then a high-pitched sound began forming a ticking pattern, like a clock. Decibels began to rise so high that the ticking sound hurt Caroline's ears. Before she could put her palms up to her ears, the sound stopped. At least they could not hear it. Both bullets imploded. The sound was dull, but the black dust and metal ricocheted off the walls of the cylinder. The sucking sound began again and the entire cylinder was clean.

No bullets.

No dust.

The tube lifted and disappeared into the ceiling. The cocoon unfolded and seemed to melt into the ceiling. Rodger slowly walked his stunned bride to the silver table and looked up at the smooth ceiling.

"No scent from the gunpowder." Rodger sniffed twice more. He was speechless.

Chapter 13

"You built that safety chamber, Sir Calvert." Rosebudial spoke in his computer dialect. "You built this lab and perfected the sundial's travel ability. After scanning your DNA, I recognize that you have traveled forward in time and perhaps do not recognize your laboratory. The future you, and present you, must never meet in the same space. You can never physically touch. Your DNA would dissipate. The lab is not your immediate concern. Caszone is attempting to kill both of you so you will never inherit this island and find the truth, which he merely suspects, about the sundial's abilities. You, Sir, in fact, have returned to calibrate the exact second Caszone's men arranged to kidnap a dynamite expert."

Rodger interjected, "A powder man?"

Rosebudial continued, "Yes. If he succeeds in kidnapping the expert, he will bring him here to build more bombs. He plans to destroy a Christian leadership convention, and then destroy Heart Island. If he discovers the time travel capabilities of the sundial, he will be the world's fiercest terrorist. Caszone's first attempt to "wipe you out" failed. He knows Caroline's father was unable to locate the exotic flower extract that he believed would cure his wife. What he did find was time travel through a wormhole here on Heart Island." Rosebudial stopped speaking, having been programmed to allow humans time to process data.

"Caroline, you are beautiful. You look like your mother, a bit exasperated. You have your father's DNA hair coloring. Your father loved you dearly. He always protects his girls."

Caroline interrupted and asked in almost a shouting voice, "Loved? He is dead? When did he die?"

"Caroline," the computerized voice of Rosebudial began", after your mother died from an incurable disease, your father, as humans say, 'lost his desire to live.' Caszone wanted to purchase the island based on old fishermen's tales. He heard of disappearances and people appearing on the island, strangely clothed, with no boats to get back to the mainland. Mr. George ignored the fables once he lost his bride. Your father did not want to deal with society so he wandered the island for several months. Barely ate, never slept, he did not try to protect himself from the elements by coming inside the unfinished mansion. When it became too cold to survive, he began sleeping in the greenhouse where he had been growing plants for your mother. There he had tried to find her cure. He hated the greenhouse where they once spent enjoyable hours. When he left the island to bury your mother, he swore only to return, to burn down the mansion. He could not look at the things he built for his family. He never returned with his two daughters."

Caroline threw both hands up to her mouth but the loud gasp escaped. "Ughwhah! Two daughters? I have a sister? Where is she? What is her name?" Tears popped from Caroline's eyes and streams began to flow down her cheeks.

"Sweet Caroline, your father called you Rosie", the low voice of the computer seemed to take on emotions, "Your sister's name is Victoria. I have been unable to locate her. I found you through the orphanage records. I set up all the necessary paperwork and waited until your wedding day to make delivery of the contracts, giving you and your husband ownership of this island. It was not necessary to find Victoria once I found the oldest heir. I will provide you with all the information I have so you and your husband can continue to look for her in your future. Right now, however, it is urgent you leave. Your older selves are returning and you must not meet."

As Rosebudial spoke, greenish-purple lights began to whirl above the sundial.

"You must go now. The robot will escort you out of the mansion. Then run to the sundial in the garden. Instructions await you there. If you fail, Caszone will destroy this island and your future. GO!" His urgency stirred their feet in the direction of the wall behind the sundial. A robot appeared and beckoned them to follow him.

They ran, following the robot as he glided just above the ground, swishing around corners like a racecar hugging a curve. After leaving the hidden corridors, racing through the house, they realized they had retraced their steps. The bookcase moved and they stepped into the library. They continued to following the robot through the mansion and into the kitchen.

When they reached the back door where they had entered earlier, Rosebudial opened his metal fist like a trap door and a sheet of yellowed notebook paper unfolded. Rodger reached out to take the paper, but the robot withdrew the paper from the open fist and handed it to Caroline.

She took the paper.

The robot did a smooth one-eighty degree turn and returned through the kitchen. Rodger and Caroline felt the dampness of the ocean and the coolness of the wind on their faces when they stepped outside. They followed the trail back to the garden. Caroline handed the note to Rodger when they reached the sundial.

Rodger quietly read the dingy note, while Caroline cautiously looked in every direction.

"Caroline", he began, "we have to return to our pasts, right now. This is a note you wrote to give to us on this date. It yellowed from the years. It says we are to hide in the wall behind the bookshelf. The one we just came through in the library. Caszone is on the property looking for us, in our pasts. He will look in the greenhouse first. We must travel through this sundial, then run to the mansion and hide in the secret wall."

Rodger lowered the brittle paper and grabbed Caroline and kissed her until she was backing away gasping for air. "I love you. Life is going to be one great adventure with you Rosebud, ugh, Rosie."

She giggled and looked down at the sundial. "You're pretty fun yourself, Mister Scent One."

They stepped onto the dial together, looked down, and began to read the words aloud. The familiar colors, the lights, the whirling garden, the smells, all began to overwhelm them as they began to travel to the past. Well, it was their present lives.

It was their lives before twins, before finding out about a younger sister.

The life they would live together was just a sundial away.

They arrived just in time to hear gruff voices heading their way. Once they were above ground, and had crawled from beneath the table, they slipped out the door, undetected by approaching footsteps. When the way seemed clear, they jetted to the mansion. The only sounds they heard were the birds chirping and the pounding of their hearts. They snuck in through the kitchen and tiptoed on the plush carpet in the hallway.

Caroline looked down to see if she could make out her earlier footprints . . . from the future.

Rodger looked at her and rolled his eyes in disbelief.

They made it, undetected, to the library. Rodger grabbed the book on the shelf, *The Sundial* and pulled with familiar strength. The bookcase moved and they slid behind the wall. Neither of them knew how long to wait, but the look in their eyes said they both were grateful to be safe. "Are you freaking out because we are hiding in our mansion on our honeymoon, or are you freaking out at the crazy information we learned today?" Rodger tried to make small talk to ease the stress level.

"I have a sister", was all she said. Rodger just shook his head.

"I saw the picture that made you faint. You age gracefully my Rosebud." Rodger had a sly smile on his face.

Caroline pinched her jeans at the hip and bowed curtsying at the waist. "You have your own lab, Sir Calvert."

They both laughed and muffled their giggles with kissing. Then there was much more kissing.

"Why couldn't our parents have had a place like this when we were dating? We could have kissed for hours, and never been found." Rodger whispered and winked.

They kissed and they waited. They waited and they kissed.

One can listen and kiss at the same time.

The realization of time travel will take time to become a realization. That is about how sane it all seemed, at the moment.

Caroline grabbed Rodger's wrist. "Please tell me we don't have to catch a killer. This Caszone is dangerous. He knows what we look like but we have no idea what he looks like or who is working for him." Caroline finished and stared at the back of the bookcase wall in front of her.

Rodger wrapped his arm around Caroline and squeezed her shoulder into his side.

"The big question is how much does Caszone know about the sundial and its time travel abilities?" Rodger finished and stared at the back of the bookcase wall. "What if he is only after the land? Maybe he wants to set up an operation here, on a deserted island."

"What if we had the advantage of stopping him before he can get to the dynamite expert?" Caroline waited on a response.

"You are a genius. You should be working investigations," Rodger said as he squeezed his wife again.

Men walked into the library chattering.

Their spines stiffened, simultaneously.

"Keep your voices down, you stupid idiots. You want the world to picnic in here so they can snack while we plot? Shut up!" One voice demanded.

"Alright already, shut up! Stop the arguing and let us get the details straight. We have to be off this island in thirty minutes. The boats will stop running the tourists, and we will have to spend the night in this creepy place," another argued.

"Limps, did you find out when and where we could nab the dynamiting powder man," the first voice asked.

"Yea, Caszone, I did. The first powder man dude killed himself instead of working for us. We found another powder man and have another opportunity at eleven o'clock tomorrow morning. A magazine called him the Weaver. We made an appointment for him to come to a wooded area and check out a new dynamiting job. On his way to check out our fake job, we will nab him at our check point." Limps explained.

"No messin' up this time. He blows this mansion down so we can get rid of the tourists and use part of this little oasis as our headquarters. Then in two weeks, we blow the biggest Christian event of the century to Hell. Did you git dat? To Hell?" Caszone laughed aloud.

"This Weaver guy better be 'dynamite' or I will have him blow *you* up." Caszone's voice was mimicking a joke, but his tone was deadly serious.

"We'll git it done, boss. We will have the dynamite, the powder man, and the kegs of beer. We will party after we waste the Weaver. Just relax and enjoy the fireworks." Limps enjoyed spelling out his cold-blooded plans.

Caszone's nod was absolute.

Rodger and Caroline were staring straight ahead, not breathing, not aware they had not exhaled throughout the men's conversation. Officer Rodger was making a mental note; 'Caszone, the leader with a gruff middle eastern accent; Limps, probably has a limp, is just a middleman, and now a third voice to add to the suspect list.'

"Caroline", Rodger started out sounding as if he was filling out a rap sheet, "A powder man is going to be kidnapped, used, and killed if we don't get a plan started right now. We should figure out how to make the sundial work for us. Two days isn't long enough to learn how to operate a time machine. That means we better figure it out and practice until we get it perfect. Once they leave we will get started."

Caroline stared at Rodger's clinched jaw and fixed eyes. "I married a detective, through and through. Thank God. I would be in a mess if you weren't in my life," Caroline said in a whimper as she laid her head on Rodger's back and wrapped her arms around his waist. They clung to one another, waiting for silence to engulf their patience.

Rodger was building up steam, ready to bolt into action.

Caroline was steadying her breathing pondering what challenging tasks they would soon face.

At least they would face them together.

The voices and footsteps faded.

Rodger turned and kissed Caroline.

"Did that kiss say, 'Partner, I love you'?" Caroline asked.

"No, it just says I love you and I am going to protect you." Rodger said as he pulled Caroline's temple into his cheek.

He felt his heart taking on newness. This cop was in unfamiliar territory. His instincts to protect his wife were stronger than he could have ever imagined. The newness was strange, and wonderful.

Chapter 14

"I don't hear anything. No voices and no shuffling feet . . . I think the mansion is empty." Caroline hoped.

"Tell that to my acid reflux," Rodger said as he pushed the bookcase wall aside, grasping Caroline's hand, and preparing to run to the sundial. They charged into the room, pushed the _Sundial_ book that closed the hidden wall, and made a mad dash to the kitchen door.

Caroline did not look at the pictures on the wall. She just focused on the fact that no one jumped out at them as they ran through the mansion. The kitchen exit was clear, and they peeked out to make sure the yard was empty of visitors and bad guys.

Caroline could pass up looking at the photos, but could not stop herself from thinking the word 'terrorists.'

"No homicidal maniacs or terrorists on my watch! We have to get to the sundial under the greenhouse." Rodger began pulling Caroline out into the open.

Caroline kept up as her long legs gobbled up ground and headed for safety. Time was the commodity they treasured and had to use wisely in order to save a man's life and insure their own futures. Without detection, they reached their destination.

There came a call for the last tourist boat of the evening.

"What do we do?" Caroline sounded panic stricken as well as out of breath.

"We let Caszone and his men leave the island. We can travel through time. Remember?" Rodger watched Caroline's face change from panic, to realization and into panic again.

"Did I marry you?" she asked.

"Ohhh yea! We got a few things to work on. But, we will do it together. One decade at a time." Rodger was being serious, but they both laughed.

Rodger glanced down at his watch. "Caroline," Rodger began, "look at the time. When we arrived on the island, it was fifteen after eleven. The tourists ate their lunch, returned, and the second load of tourists came, ate their snacks in the garden and now they are leaving, right?" Rodger asked.

"No, I believe this is the same group that came for lunch." Caroline clipped her bottom lip beneath her front teeth.

"That would mean time did not pass while we were traveling into the future. Does that sound right?" Rodger thought, "rhetorical question, move on."

Caroline did not seem confident, but she tried. "We need to look for the next instructions. They must be here, inside the greenhouse. Look around."

Rodger turned in a circle, looking in every direction. Soon he knew they would need to descend into the gloomy underground tomb. Further instructions eluded them so they prepared to climb below. Caroline spotted an unusual picture dangling from a long nail on the framework of the greenhouse. It was a picture of a single white rosebud.

"Typically white roses are given to brides or to a woman whose mother is deceased on Mother's Day. Can you reach that picture? I want to look at it a little closer." Caroline pointed and Rodger stretched upward, pulled the nail out, and placed the framed photo into Caroline's waiting palms. Turning the picture over Caroline pulled the tabs loose and removed the contents, glass, and all. There were several yellowed sheets behind a piece of cardboard backing.

It was a handwritten message from Caroline's mother.

"My dearest daughters, Caroline and Victoria, I love you both dearly. I am too ill to move into our new home on Heart Island. I know your father will care for you both, as he loves you both dearly. My twin sister, Margaret Caszone, lives in Spartanburg, South Carolina. If you

need to rest or need comforting please plan a vacation with dear Margaret. She also promised me she would come to Heart Island, and help you settle in your new home. I will not be able to help with your graduation, your wedding dresses, or hold my grandchildren. I have great pleasure in knowing my family will stay together in such a beautiful home filled with love. Create many wonderful memories together. Take care of your father, George. He was the first of God's great gifts to me. Daddy says that butterflies cannot move their wings because time stands still when the four of us are together in God's garden of love. You two beautiful daughters complete my life. We will be reunited in Heaven's mansion. Trust in God and one day we will walk together in God's garden. I love you both dearly. Your mother, Louise, "Butterfly".

When Caroline finished reading the letter aloud, she slumped to the ground. She was too stunned to cry and too stunned to faint. "I hadn't noticed that single picture there before. Do you think I came back in time while we were in the house and nailed it up there for us to find later?" Caroline asked with eyebrows scrunched together into one line. "I am exasperated. I don't think I am breathing." Caroline put her head between her knees, just in case. She sure did not want to pass out and miss anything now.

Rodger took the letter from her hands and reread every word carefully. "Caroline," Rodger began", Listen to this, 'Daddy says that butterflies cannot move their wings because time stands still when the four of us are together in God's garden of love,' do you think that is what the robot meant by finding our instructions here?"

That is when Caroline began to sob. She did not make a sound, just sobbed. Her shoulders heaved up and down and the air moistened with her tears and warm breath. "She said that we completed her life", Caroline gasped.

Rodger did not say a word; he just knelt and put his arms around his wife. "She wants us to live on Heart Island, not just a year, but she wants us to raise our children here."

Caroline raised her head up so fast she almost hit Rodger in the nose. "Victoria, we have to find her. We have an Aunt. Maybe Victoria lives with Aunt Margaret. It is possible. Somehow, we were separated. I went to the orphanage. Margaret Caszone. That is why he is trying to get ownership of the island. He knew something of the legends of time travel. That means Dad knew something about the sundial before Mama died. Else he wouldn't have said that about the butterfly wings standing still." Caroline was on her feet. "Let's check out the sundial again." Caroline said moving a plant aside and getting ready to crawl beneath the table.

Rodger was right behind her, still holding the only connection Caroline possessed from her mother. When they reached the underground sundial Rodger put his free hand on Caroline's shoulder. It took his firm grip to stop her in her tracks.

Chapter 15

"Rosebud," Rodger stood his ground, "are you realizing that the man who tried to scare you, maybe even kill you, is your Uncle?"

Caroline did not say anything for a few spine-tingling moments. "Yes, I do," Caroline continued, "but we have a man's life to save and perhaps our own future as well."

Once below, in the damp underground tomb, Caroline bent to look at the sundial and saw a tiny carving of a butterfly in its roughly hewn stone. She reached to her neckline and pulled the chain, hosting the butterfly necklace from beneath her shirt. What little light was flickering into the cold tomb caught on the corners of the butterfly, and a rainbow of lights bounced around the damp dirt walls and onto the face of the sundial.

The room seemed to illuminate with light. Eerie at first, then greater with whiter flickers and an intense bounce like a strobe light.

Rodger unlocked the necklace and Caroline placed the butterfly into the sundial's face. It found a perfect fit at twelve o'clock.

Caroline stood and watched the tomb walls fade as light, carpet and furniture engulfed the space.

"My darling daughter, "A beautiful woman with honey colored hair draped around her pale face stood from a chair and walked forward, making her appear to stand right in front of Caroline, "If we are meeting, you have used the butterfly locket to open this hologram. I am assuming you are Caroline and you have recently married. To continue this conservation you must answer a few questions. Do so quickly before this hologram discontinues. There will be a bonus question just in case you might not know the answers."

A keyboard flashed up between the two women. "Caroline, use the keyboard in front of you to type in the answers. George says that we are not interacting, but responding by programming the computer. Place your hands on the alphabets and we can begin. Question number one. What was the name of the man who brought you the paperwork concerning Heart Island?"

Caroline did not hesitate. She quickly typed Emanuel Bishop.

"Question number two. What is your sister's name?" Caroline's birth mother waited for the answer by putting a fist up to her delicate lips. In anticipation, she could only pray that Caroline had found out about her sister from George's computer.

Caroline's eyes swelled with pools of tears as she whispered, "Her name is Victoria." Warming tears rolled down her cheeks as she typed her sister's name. It seemed to complete a circle or fill a void within her.

"The third question should be easy. The only way you could have found out the name of your sister was to hear it from George's computerized robot. The third test is for you to tell me the computer's name."

Pinched lips were hiding behind the fists she brought to her mouth. As soon as Caroline opened her mouth to speak, little corners crept from behind the white knuckles, and a smile began to emerge on the other side of time. The sheer joy that spread over Mrs. George Boldt's face was a sight Caroline and Rodger would never forget.

"The computer's name is Rose-bud-dial," Caroline carefully typed in the name. "Like dialing the past using a rose," Caroline said slowly chancing a look at the sundial beneath her feet.

"This is your bonus question. What rare flower do you think your father researched to find a cure for my disease?"

Caroline thought of the beakers and research they had seen in the greenhouse. She typed O-r-c-h-i-d.

"If you are still hearing my voice and seeing my image, or rather, this hologram, then you are indeed my daughter Caroline, the heir to Heart Island." Mrs. Boldt sat down again. She looked as if she was tired, but that the weight of the world had fallen from her dainty shoulders.

"I knew you would become a horticulturist. I could see the love for plants in the way you touched each petal, each root. I somehow believed you would turn out to be like your mother. I love you, dear daughter."

Caroline staggered as she took in a gasp that they shared through time and space. Neither more powerful than love.

"Dear, your father says this hologram will only last a short time but we agreed we should record this message for you. I welcome your husband into our family with great joy. I know he was sent to you through my prayers of love."

Caroline gasped again when her mother said the word 'sent'.

"I do hope you will remember how much your father, sister and I love you. I am ill. I will miss all the important days I should be spending with you. All I have time to say is that I love you deeply. I pray every day for you and your little sister, Victoria. You father says this hologram thing will be a commonly used item in the twenty-first century. How he plans to put it on the island, where you can find it, is beyond me. Darling, please enjoy the island. Your father says it holds great secrets to life. I do not believe I will live long enough to move in, but when the three of you do move in, please take care of the gardens and especially the sundial. Put your hand here against my palm and follow it with yours."

Caroline watched her mother extend her thin arms and put her palm up facing Caroline's. Lifting her shaky hand, she placed her palm against her mothers. The colors shot out from around the hologram as Caroline and her mother's hand lightly touched. George stepped in with a stool and put it in front of her mother. Kneeling on the stool, she bent at the waist and leaned forward. Caroline followed with her own hand, palm outward, and they kept traveling toward the sundial underneath Caroline.

"That is your father, Caroline." Rodger whispered. "I recognize him from the portrait in the mansion." Rodger was watching Caroline as her expression never changed, both waiting to see what Caroline's hand was about to reveal.

When her mother reached the carpet on the floor, she pointed with her index finger, looking up at George to make sure she was being accurate.

George explained, "Rosie, Caroline, right here. Touch that spot on the sundial where your mother is pointing. She is too exasperated to record anything else, dear. I love you Caroline."

Another gasp came out of Caroline with such a whooshing sound that she scared herself.

"That is my Dad's voice! Look at him. He looks so strong!" Caroline put her finger into a dirt-filled area on the sundial and felt the dust and sod give way. She blew the dirt aside. A rose emblem, imbedded into the metal, gracefully unfolded as if it were blooming from under the dirt.

Dirt and time had rusted the rose. Caroline, shaken, looked up at Rodger and whispered her nicknames, "Rosebud, Rosie".

Even in the daylight, one might miss seeing the tiny detail. As soon as her fingertip disappeared into a small opening at the center of the rose, the hologram was gone. Family faces and voices were still alive in the damp, darkened air of the underground tomb. It was as if the sundial had united generations through one whisper in the span of a moment.

Caroline tumbled onto half of the dirt floor and half of the sundial. "They were beautiful. I saw my parents. I really saw them, heard them." Caroline was so overwhelmed with emotion she let all of the fear from the last few days, all of the emotional build-up of wedding preparations, and all of the years she lost not knowing her true family. More than tears mingled with the dirt. Rodger knelt and held Caroline as she trembled from past to present.

Several healing minutes washed over her before she regained her focus and smiled up at Rodger. "Your father said, 'exasperated', just like you do."

She giggled like a schoolchild. She had seen her parents. She had heard their voices. She began to laugh aloud.

Before long they both laughed so hard, they began to cry. "The craziest thing is, we can't tell anyone about the hologram. Your father missed it by a few decades or centuries. We have the technology, but we do not go around leaving E-mail hologram downloads." Rodger laughed out every word. Caroline began to laugh even harder at her techno husband.

Caroline jumped to her feet, wiped her face of dirt and tears, and her eyes became so large they looked scary to Rodger. "Dad traveled, through time. The sundial is a means of time travel. If he successfully traveled then we can too. That rose on the sundial has to be the key." Caroline narrowed her eyes as she jumped back down on all fours and began looking at the embedded rose.

"Stand up Rosebud, let's try to say the words on the sundial again and then put your finger into the rose and see what happens." Rodger was trying to figure out what, if anything was radiating from her eyes this time. A few minutes silently ticked away as they looked past each other into the darkness, absorbing all the possibilities.

"Ohhhkay. I do not have a better idea. Let's try. Will we be able to travel forward and backwards in time? Both?" Caroline asked but her eyes darted off past Rodger, again, transcending the earthen wall.

"We should try the past first and not go too far back. Try a recent event that we can remember. Will we be living the past or will we be looking at ourselves living in the past?" Rodger let a few minutes pass. "What do you want to do?" Rodger waited.

"Why not go back to the day we met?" Caroline asked. "That might be too far back on our first try. Why not try just a few minutes ago, while we were viewing the hologram?" Rodger decided.

"Ohhhkkay. I guess that-that will bbbee okay." Caroline stuttered. She wasn't sure she could experience it all again.

"Remember, if we are looking at ourselves watching the hologram, do not touch the past, ugh, us. I am sure we cannot occupy the same space at the same time. Here we go. First, we stand, and then together recite the writing on the sundial. Then you put your finger inside the little rose medallion and hope we can figure out how to maneuver the time. I hope we will know the difference between dialing the past and the future. I hope it is exact." Rodger held Caroline by the waist and stood behind her looking over her head at the coded words around the sundial, just beneath them.

"Here we go. Hold on Rosebud." Rodger whispered in her ear as he prepared to read the words on the sundial. "Together . . . ready on one, two, three . . . **'Today is yesterday without fear. Dial tomorrow while it is near. Lock yourself inside before the**

three collide. Salvage life in the bud before the darkening of the Scud.'"

They finished reading the face of the sundial and the blue whirling colors and strange sounds engulfed them as they had before. Caroline pushed her finger into the rose emblem. A keyboard with numbers and letters appeared in front of them, hovering like the hologram had earlier. Rodger placed his fingers on the keyboard and typed in the month, date, year, and Heart Island, then guessing he typed 'The Sundial'. The keyboard disappeared and Rodger rammed the big key into the grooved slot as he had before. The colors in the room stopped.

The hologram appeared just above their heads and they watched themselves experiencing their own history.

Caroline gasped; a deep guttural sound followed. Instead of watching herself, she once again watched her parents and listened to their messages for their daughter. As soon as the hologram disappeared, Caroline bent and stuck her finger into the rose emblem and the blue translucent lights whirled again. Rodger reached for the big sundial key, pulling it out of the rutted fixture.

Everything stopped except for the pounding heartbeats in the chests of the time travelers. The silence lasted too long but neither noticed.

"Did we just travel back in time and travel forward in time to the present moment?" asked Rodger in bewildering state of mind.

"Cop mode just kicked in. If we have inherited what I think we just inherited and it works, we have a responsibility to protect this knowledge. Caroline, do you hear me?" Rodger asked.

"Yea, Scent One, I should say we both have been sent for such a time as this. Do you remember how God chose Esther to become a queen just at the right time to spare God's people? You were not only sent into my life, but God planned for you to be the Scent One to help me with your skills to best operate and handle this responsibility. Dad knew I was going to marry a police officer. He had to have known your investigative skills." Caroline turned and put her arms around her husband.

"With or without time travel the human heart seems to sketch the details of important moments on your heart, as if it were a pallet. I feel like the artist of time is detailing our futures right now," Caroline whispered.

This would be a defining moment for each of them. Futures depended on whether or not they would share this knowledge or destroy the sundial forever.

Chapter 16

"I wish I had backup," Rodger said looking off into space.

"We have made an awesome discovery. We are going to have to be each other's backup if we plan to keep this from the world." Caroline said, staring into the future somewhere past the space she and Rodger shared.

"We have to deal with Caszone first. I need to do a background search on him and his associates. We cannot stop him if we do not know what he knows. You do realize that if we can find Victoria we can never tell her what part we play in stopping Caszone's plans." Rodger was looking at Caroline and waiting for a nod or some acknowledgment of their agreement. Caroline finally nodded yes. Rodger took her by the hand and they climbed out of the quickly cooling underground tomb.

Night was wrapping its dark arms around the island. The last boat would be waiting to take them back to the mainland. Caszone could be waiting to take them out, permanently.

No boat was in sight. They would have to spend the night on the island rather than risk using the cell phone and asking for a boat to return.

"I will use the computer in the library. That way I can erase my research from the hard drive", Rodger began his planning as they scoped out the empty gardens. Huddled together against the biting cool breeze sweeping over the island from the Saint Lawrence Seaway, they made their way to their mansion. Rodger jiggled the keys in his hand, finding the kitchen door key. They carefully walked as they listened for voices and sounds.

All was quiet. They made their way to the library. Rodger turned on the computer, got online, and did a search on Caszone. Nothing looked like a match.

"Why not search for the powder man? Did he call him a weaver? Google 'Weaver' and 'dynamite'." Caroline was still giving her advice when Rodger swiveled the leather chair around and gave her a look of surprise.

"What? Don't be surprised! I have learned from the best in a very short time." Caroline put her hand on her hip and turned her eyes to the ceiling.

"Oh, so that is how it is going to be. Just don't ask me to wallow in the mud when planting-season rolls around. You can play cop all you want. Actually, you are right. I will search for the good guys first." Rodger said, rolling his eyes up at his looming wife.

Caroline softly laughed at his copycat gesture.

Rodger typed in 'News Report Dynamite Powder Man Commits Suicide'. He hit the search button. An article appeared with a picture of Jason Marcus under the title: Powder Man Leaves Legacy. Rodger clicked print and reached for the paper tray. Then he copied the article for his office and team of investigators. After typing several email addresses into the outgoing box, he pasted the article and hit the send button. Then he typed a message to each of the men he had selected, including one specialist with the FBI, and told them to find out where the powder man would be traveling. Rodger warned the officers that the men were armed terrorists.

"It appears from the article that the target goes by The Weaver and possibly is the son of the deceased powder man, Jason Marcus."

"Did you delete all the search information?" Caroline asked, still amazed at the quick response time of the investigators.

"Yes, Caroline, I pulled all the roots right out of the ground." Caroline nodded and kept looking over Rodger's shoulder at all the messages stacking on top of each other.

"Men inside Weaver's office. Found calendar and location. Tomorrow meet. Men working location. Found wooded area in bend of road, gulley on either side, footprints. Found possible target area. Setting stakeout in the trees. Should we confirm?" Rodger responded.

"No confirmation. Low profile here. I will call FBI locator cell number later to confirm. What time was hit predicted?" Rodger finished typing.

"Eleven o'clock A.M. tomorrow. Out."

Rodger typed and said 'Out.'

"Professional," Caroline said as she stood to straighten her back. "I had no idea you guys talked on email like you do on those walkie-talkies."

"Just habit, I suppose." Rodger said as he wiped out all records of his ever having used the computer. He folded the paper that he had printed into a small piece and shoved it into his shoe.

"That is different," squeaked Caroline.

"It's exasperating." Rodger said smiling up at her as he stood. "Now", Rodger began without blinking, "My Princess of the mansion, it looks like we need to find a place to bed down for the night."

"Oohh," Caroline blushed, "We do have to spend our first night sleeping in our mansion, don't we?"

"Is Sir Rodger the same as Prince Rodger?" He asked, making them both laugh.

They needed to get back to the honeymooners they started out to be just a few days ago. They walked away from the library and headed upstairs to find a comfortable royal bed to sleep in.

Bed, they found.

Sleep eluded them.

Rodger knew he had to construct a plan before morning. Caszone, or his men, would eventually find them no matter if they stayed in the area or returned. If they fled, then the Weaver would lose his life after blowing up Heart Island. The terrorists would set up their command post thousands of Christians would be murdered during their event.

No sleep for Rodger.

His men, along with his FBI buddy, Robert Mason, would be working tonight. He could do no less.

After Caroline drifted off to sleep, Rodger sat outside their beautifully decorated room, listening, thinking, and praying. Trying to imagine living in this mansion, and raising children with Caroline was beyond wonderful. Decisions had to be made about the sundial's time travel abilities. Perilous potential.

Paradoxes and historical disasters.

Way too much to think ahead about right now. Rodger had a terrorist, a powder man, an island, Christians, and most of all, his beautiful wife to consider protecting.

How could he protect them? He whispered to himself, "What do I have to work with? I need a bargaining chip. Something to get Caszone's greedy mind distracted before destroying his plans. Rodger leaned against the door frame leading to the luxurious master bedroom, almost dozing off, when it hit right in his gut.

"The legend! That is it! I will just tell Caszone the truth. Why not let him *be* the test pilot? Yeah!" Rodger shot his fist into the air with victory on his lips. He locked the bedroom door behind him, slid between the satin sheets, beside Caroline, and fell asleep like a prince.

Rodger woke up first and stared down into Caroline's innocent face. She radiated love.

She must have felt him staring down at her because she rolled over, stretched, and then shot straight up looking around at the room. "I forgot. I was just getting ready to smile thinking about sleeping beside you again, all night, and snap, here I am in a princess bed with my handsome prince." Caroline smiled up at Rodger.

"Look up at the canopy," Rodger whispered, "I didn't notice last night that the sheers draped over the walnut posts are decorated with tiny red rosebuds." Rodger said pulling his Rosebud closer to him.

"I think I came up with a plan. We could just wait right here in bed for Caszone's men to find us. They will eventually. Might as well relax." Rodger stretched out and Caroline was climbing over him to get to the door and run for safety.

"Get up; they might come back here since we didn't leave on the tour boat. I am sure they watched for the boat to bring us back. They have to know we stayed on the island." Caroline was frantic.

"Relax, we want them to find us. That is part of my plan." As Rodger was speaking, the door burst open, breaking the lock, and in walked Caszone, Limps and a tough looking muscle guy. Limps was an American. The other two men looked just like they had sounded, foreign. Caroline stood beside Rodger in disbelief that the plan was underway, this early in the morning.

"Well, well, if it isn't the owners test driving the tourist spot." Caszone said in a cold voice, cigar hanging from his lips.

"Good morning. I am Rodger Calvert. I think we better fix that door before the tour continues." Rodger said as he stood to shield his wife with his body.

"No tours today, Rodger," Caszone began, "The boats had a little misfortune last night, sank, all except the one we brought. We sent it back. No one will be touring or leaving this island until we give the orders. Got that, Rodger?"

Caszone was flabby, just like Rodger suspected. Limps did limp, just a little, on his left side. The muscle looked like he would not know how to get out of a pair of handcuffs using the key, as the men often said at the precinct. Rodger felt confident that he had evaluated the men without seeing them. Now, to divide and conquer.

First, Rodger had to bait the snare. "What is your name?" Rodger asked.

"Caszone. Today is your lucky day, Rodger; you get to take me on a tour of this island."

Rodger responded, "I am not sure I want to walk around this spooky island. I have heard too many tales. I have seen too many graves of men who tried to tour this island. Not so sure I want to stay here too long, either."

"What have you heard about this island, Rodger?" Caszone began his interrogation, hoping to find something of truth about the tales and fables he too had heard and even researched.

"Some said it was haunted." Caszone moved to the side of the big wooden poster bed where Rodger was sitting. Rodger cut his eyes to Caroline and motioned for her to sit in a chair next to him. She moved toward the chair and Caszone said nothing, allowing her to sit near her husband.

Caszone demanded, raising his voice, "Tell me what you have heard!" His demeanor changed from that of power to an evil, hungry glare. Greed was in his heart, which gave Rodger what he knew he needed to execute his plan.

Rodger's training included optimizing his enemy's weaknesses in order to quickly take control. In this case, it was more than controlling; it had become life or death.

He would not consider it an option to let anything happen to Caroline. His protective instincts scared him into sharpening his attention on the take-down plan. So far, Caszone did not seem to need violence in order to assert his authority. Good sign he might be a negotiator. Rodger's specialty training included negotiation. He had seen kidnappings, suicide attempts, and stand offs with cops where his skills turned the situation around to the favor of the United States Police Force.

Rodger was ready.

All he had to do now was protect Caroline and get those men underground.

The sundial would do the rest.

"Disappearances, men showing up from nowhere with odd clothing, even heard that ghosts roam the island at night," Rodger gave his information and watched Limps' eyes widen at the thought of ghosts. Rodger held back a laugh by swallowing, hard.

Caroline noticed and shot him a mischievous nod.

Caszone lost control of the conversation and his directives were taken away from him little by little. Once he moved the party to the kitchen downstairs, he slammed his fist down on the counter top and paused, waiting for the silence to snap the group's heads in his direction. It worked just the way he planned.

"You are burning daylight", Caszone said, wrinkling his forehead and scrunching his brow, yet another effort to intimidate Rodger. Instead of fixing his eyes on Caszone, Rodger looked at Caroline and saw her fearful eyes. Without changing his demeanor, he waited for Caroline to look at him instead of Caszone. Rodger shifted his weight, dropped his arm down by his side, and patted the outside of his leg until he saw that Caroline recognized what the sign language meant. He was still packing. Caszone had not searched for weapons.

Caroline did not drop her eyes to his leg, and especially not to his ankle, but Rodger's confidence builder worked. She could feel her blood pressure dropping back, down to normal. Their gazes slid back to Caszone.

His facial expression had not changed, but the atmosphere in the kitchen did. Rodger chose a sweet bun from the display case and handed it to Limps. "Would you like something?" Rodger asked with no emotion in his voice.

"Nuuugh, no thank you, man. I'm ugh," he rattled on, glancing at Caszone", I'm, ugh, cool." Limps clearly did not operate well under stress.

"Now," Rodger thought to himself, "we all know Wimpy Limpy won't be giving us any trouble. Plan operative number one, Divide and Conquer."

Chapter 17

Caszone stiffened his shoulders and walked toward the dining room. Without turning around, he said to the muscle man, "Bring them here".

Caszone pushed the doors aside as he stomped into the elaborately decorated dining room. The serene scent of oak, mahogany, and fabrics releasing the aroma of candles, clashed with the pushing and shoving that went on as Mr. Muscle asserted his place in the chain of authority. Once inside, the pushing stopped, and everyone froze in their tracks, their shoes making impressions on the combed carpet. Each waited on the mastermind to give his orders.

Caszone pulled back a heavy drape, filling his fist with velvety golden cording, and looked out the window. He wasn't looking at anything in particular. He seemed to mysteriously withdraw himself from the situation, leaving an empty shell of a body. With a dull thud, his head landed on the glass pane. Limps stepped forward as if he were going to check on his boss. He stopped himself and froze with one foot forward.

Silence turned the room into a tomb. Rodger thought for a moment that perhaps his men had docked Heart Island and he had missed the whooshing sound from the silencer on a sharp shooter's gun. He looked at Caszone for blood. Rodger saw no signs of anything that might be causing his paralysis.

"Limps", Caszone began with a quiet voice, "What time is it?" Caszone stayed in his awkward position.

"It, ugh, it, it is ten minutes after ten, ugh, sir, Mr. Caszone." Limps pulled his foot right back to the exact spot where he had been indenting the carpet before Caszone went a little whacky. It was a perfect fit.

Caszone didn't move but screamed so loud it should have cracked the glass in the window. "SIT DOWN!" Caroline and Rodger rushed to pull out the heavy oak chairs. Limps and muscle man did the same. Caszone finally moved. When he did, his eyes caught the site of muscle man sitting at the table and he flung himself across the room, fists in the air.

Muscle man did not see it coming. His back was to Caszone. The look on Caroline's face must have given it away. Muscle man dodged his head to the right and Caszone's fist all but splintered the great oak chair back. He recoiled his fist and punched muscle man under his chin. His knuckles continued upward and scraped his nostrils. Caszone screamed into muscle man's face, "YOU do NOT sit unless I tell you to! Do you understand?"

Fighting hard not to wipe his bloody nose, muscle man said, "Yeah, boss".

Rodger made a mental note: "If they look like they might try to lay a finger on Caroline, aim carefully. Don't plan to fight either of them."

Caszone walked to the table and punched his fist between Limps and Rodger. "I know you have been on this island long enough to realize that you will not survive living here one year. I am not leaving until my plans are completed. Since you know more than you should, I need to-how do the cops say it-extract some information. Yea, extract. I need to know what you know. What did you find here? You keep risking your life to stay here so I want to know why!" Caszone finished his extracting method of staring Rodger down. Straightening, stretching, and rolling his shoulders, Caszone then flung his bloody fist around as if to give it better circulation. Once again, he stood in silence. It was as if he were preparing to either control himself or lose his temper and go on a slaughtering rampage.

Rodger knew he was trying to figure out what questions he wanted to ask. It was then that Rodger knew the mad man had no idea what existed under the greenhouse. Caszone would be wild with the knowledge of traveling through time and ruling the world with his power and greed. What Caszone did not know was that Rodger knew all about the eleven o'clock attack to kidnap the powder man in a wooded area.

"Caroline and I found the treasure." Rodger said without looking at Caroline. He hoped she would figure out what he was doing and play along. She stiffened and wiggled in the soft comfortable cushions on the dining room chairs. She was ready and she trusted her Scent One. "Show him the key, Rosebud. I put it in your pocket this morning." Rodger pointed to her vest where the sundial key was visible to every eye in the room.

The astonishment on Limps' face was classic to Rodger's investigative training.

Several minutes passed before Caszone seemed to be able to take in a breath. When he did, the other men filled their lungs along with him.

They were in harmony.

It was eerie.

"Rodger, get up. You are going to take me to the treasure. Limps, you stay here with Caroline. Lock her in one of the rooms with a key hanging out of the knob if you have to." Caszone began delegating his manipulative plans.

Rodger slowly stood, pushed his chair under the table, frowning said, "Caszone, I need Caroline to go with us. She has the other half of the key. Codes only she understands will open the treasure. I do not know the codes. We need her. Might as well not go if we don't take her with us."

Rodger prayed under his breath for Caszone to agree. If he left her here, he would send the muscle man to kill her, and they both knew it.

Caszone did not give away any expressions as to what he was considering. They could tell the wheels in his brain were turning. He was weighing the options and considering what Rodger might be planning. You could almost smell the singe of little hairs burning in Caszone's ears. Rodger saw the confusion on muscle man's face and Caszone's inability to make quick decisions, so he took control of the situation, just as he had been trained in Tactical Maneuvers classes.

"Caszone, if you leave her here she will steal the other half of the treasure. We hid it here in the mansion. She won't need a key. We take her and the key and you get both treasures."

Rodger was good, but his skills had never depended upon saving the life of his wife before now.

Time was getting short. All the arguing was exactly what Rodger needed to stall. He wanted to get Caszone and his men in place at the exact moment, else time travel would be revealed, and a shootout, imminent.

Caroline was too sweet and innocent to see the horror Rodger knew would follow in a burst of angry drama and bloodshed. He would go for his ankle gun if they insisted on leaving Caroline behind with Limps.

Rodger had a feeling his men were around. He was praying they didn't barge in and try to do a take down. He did not want them to know about the time traveling sundial. It was all too risky. Little prickly hairs would stand up on his neck when he knew the locked and loaded teams were nearby.

He would protect Caszone as if he was taking him hostage. Rodger knew he had to get the men to the sundial, no matter what. Caszone agreed they would return for the treasure inside the mansion later. Caszone seemed to be dragging time out now instead of the hurried pace he had tried to set with his fists.

Rodger predicted people's moves, examined motives, and those skills were earning him a reputation for being the top requested negotiator in the United States. He used his guns when necessary but he never liked the outcome.

"Death doesn't solve anything," Rodger had said in his last police academy speech. "Reforming the villain into society to become a productive citizen will always outweigh the price of a casket and an empty chair in a home. Remember, if your bullet misses, you become the target and the suspect becomes a hero to the cult leaders you will face in the next generation." Rodger was looking into the face of someone who had followed a wronged cult leader and wanted his dues.

"Oh, yes sir, Caszone will get his due reward. Right around eleven o'clock," Rodger thought while guiding his countenance into neutral.

Chapter 18

The parade began outside, through the dining room, through the kitchen, and out the back door. The walk was rather short to the greenhouse but the steps difficult to balance while looking around for snipers. Multitasking was just one of Rodger's training skills he used in his unbalanced world every day. Watching his wife of less than one week trust him with both of their lives was overwhelming. He did not know how to describe the wrenching knot in his chest except to compare it with the real fear he knew he would live with should time travel end up in the hands of a man like Caszone. A Christian event about to be bombed might not even have gotten to the planning stages if Caszone went back in time and destroyed its leadership.

It was that thought that shook Rodger into reality. "My faith. Caroline's faith. The people we are and the couple we make together is all because of what Jesus Christ did when He faced fear and death. He knew He was God's son and still He was willing to die for every man's sin. Jesus faced death in order to give life. His life made a bridge for man and God to connect, once again, in fellowship. I am dealing with men who have sinned and have never turned their lives over to God. It is my faith in Jesus and my love for mankind that will get us through the next minutes of our lives."

Rodger was deep in thought as he scanned the parameter. Then he began to pray, "I thank you Heavenly Father that you will give me the strength to do what I must do to ensure the safety of many. I may never understand why you chose Caroline and why you chose me to make these choices today, but I will obey Your guidance. Protect Caroline and forgive us for our sins. I love you Jesus. Amen."

They reached the greenhouse and Caroline's mind was awhirl. She had an idea what Rodger might be going to try to do, but it would be tricky. Caroline was looking left and right. Rodger looked at his watch. Caroline was wondering if any of Rodger's men had heard about the boats sinking. They could be at Heart Island by now. They would probably swim to the coast, if the waters were not too rapid. Instead of looking for a knight in shining armor, she opted to trust God to speak to Rodger and give him the best plan for getting out of this mess.

Caroline prayed, "Lord, I have struggled all my life to push aside the visions and confusing dreams about who I really am and where I came from. Now that I have found the truth, the responsibility is overwhelming. I have a wonderful husband. If it were not for his training, we probably would not be alive right now. I will never complain about his job. I have a sister I need to find. I have to live here on Heart Island for a year so our family can inherit this miracle and fulfill your plan for our lives. Lord, all I ask is that you give Rodger your grace and show him what to do. I know he does not want to kill those men. Neither does he want the powder man to be murdered. Please show him your perfect way. Thank you, Heavenly Father. I love you, Jesus. Holy Spirit, I thank you for being Rodger's teacher and for being his guide at this moment. Amen."

Rodger moved the table to the side and lifted the flooring. The dampness of the earth's tomb hit them in the face with its coolness. Caszone jumped in first, taking Caroline's hand, and helping her down. Then Rodger jumped into the small space. Limps sat down and slid along the cool, crumbly wall. When muscle man crammed his way in, he took up the rest of the breathing space.

Rodger took the small flashlight he had stuffed behind his belt loop, out, and looked at Caroline. She rolled her eyes. She knew his officers had been on the island and left some items during the night. At some point Rodger had left her alone in the mansion and retrieved only God knew what from their stash.

"I found this little light in one of the kitchen drawers, yesterday." Rodger rolled his eyes, mocking Caroline's.

Caroline said aloud, "Oh boy! Here we go. This is exasperating!"

Rodger looked at his watch through the tiny light beam. "Caszone, I need to unlock the, ugh, laser light beams first. I need you and the men to help with the weight distribution. Caroline and I have not been able to get to the treasure because we needed something heavy enough yet small enough to stand on the face of the sundial. The three of you men together should make up the difference." Rodger said, watching their faces to see if they bought his line.

They did.

They moved, shoving, and getting off balance, but in the end, they shared the space.

"I will say some words with Caroline, which will voice activate the system. You will see the laser lights before we insert Caroline's sundial key right between your feet. Then a keyboard will flash up in front of where I will be standing. I will type in the secret code and Caroline will insert her finger right there beside Limps' foot. Then you will be amazed at the treasure you will see." Rodger finished his directions and they looked like stunned deer on a racetrack.

Without waiting for an explanation or questions as to how Rodger learned all this in a few days on the Island, they just stood there, motionless.

Together, Caroline and Rodger whispered, "Weird".

Rodger thought of Daniel in the Lion's den. "The look on the faces of the lions must have been horror when they couldn't open their mouths. That is what these Cowardly Lions look like." Humph, Rodger whispered to himself thinking about the Emerald City of forest and trees they were about see.

It was one-minute until eleven o'clock.

Rodger and Caroline stood, holding hands in a semi-circle around the terrorists. Everyone looked down at the symbols illuminated by the handy light. With the first word spoken the men all took a cold gasp as they watched the symbols melt into the alphabet. Rodger and Caroline were reading, *"Today is yesterday, without fear.*

Dial tomorrow while it is near. Lock yourself inside before the three collide. Salvage life in the bud before the darkening of the Scud."

Lights twirled, blue invaded what air space was available inside the stuffy tomb, and Rodger lunged down to the opening crevice and inserted the sundial key. The holographic keyboard appeared and Caroline pushed Limp's dirty shoe aside to insert the butterfly necklace at the rosebud.

The men were trying to take it all in. Caszone could not turn his head about quick enough. Rodger was punching in the time, location, and digitized coordinates that he had asked his men to get for him during the night. He had that information stored in his other shoe. He checked for accuracy and hit the send button.

Greenery came into view and seemed to replace the earthen walls about them. Rodger lunged down, grabbed Caroline by the neckline, and pulled her to the wall. Rodger caught a glimpse through the trees of a silver flash so he reached inside the whirl of lights and gave Caszone's shoulder a shove to his right.

Everything went dark. Pitch black.

Caroline and Rodger could not see their hands in front of their faces. The air smelled like smoke. Neither spoke for a moment.

"Scud," Rodger surmised. "That smell is what a Scud missile smells like when one has been destroyed. They do not smell that way when they detonate, just when they have imploded and lose their explosive power. The Christian event was set to be bombed with a Scud. I hadn't thought of that being the meaning on the sundial." Rodger slid down the dirt wall, his arm around his wife, and sighed. They sat there a moment, until Rodger started to click his tiny flashlight off and on, off and on, off . . . and Caroline took it from him.

"Life with you is going to be exasperating, but fun."

As they stood, the sundial made a clunk-clunk sound, and turned on its own like a combination on a vault. After three turns, they crept over to look at it as it settled into the dirt. The coded symbols had completely changed.

Rodger grabbed his wife and pulled her to his chest.

Looking deeply into her eyes he smiled and said, "Another day, Caroline Boldt Calvert, for we have a honeymoon to complete, a sister to find, and packing to do when we get home." Rodger and Caroline Calvert kissed and climbed out of the time travel womb. Once they covered the floor and moved the table into place Rodger could hear familiar radios just outside the greenhouse door.

They walked out together and the crowd of men cheered. Some were in scuba diving gear, some were in uniform, and some looked like tourists. One of the men walked up to Rodger and slapped him on the back and handed him a "secure radio" as they called it.

"Yes sir, this is Officer Rodger Calvert. Over," he said as he let go of the microphone switch. "Three men. Caszone is the big guy with the busted knuckles. Limps is the little scraggly dude, but we were unable to secure any information on the muscle man. Over."

"Yes sir, terrorists. The Christian event the world is talking about. Over."

"Oh. Both of them? Over."

"They had the Scud with them? While they were picking up the powder man? Over."

"Then Limps' leg w-a-s the Scud. Over."

"No mercy from men with no heart. How is the powder man, sir? Over."

"Thank God! Thank you, Officer Mason. Over."

"Yes sir, we will. Over."

Officer Rodger handed the secure line back to the officer in charge. All three men were dead. The power man was safe. A job well done, on his honeymoon, just earned him an extra week off.

Smelling the scents of the island and letting the breeze wash over them the Calverts were already at home. Many decisions were ahead of them but the next few days would be relaxing, fun, and stress free.

Caroline turned to look at the greenhouse and felt a nudge. "Rosebud, Rosie, I love you," Rodger swooned. Rodger turned to watch the scuba diving experts loading their tanks onto the dingy boats they had rented, when he got a nudge.

"Scent One, I love you," Caroline said as she saw a glimpse of her future in Rodger's warming eyes.

A life filled with love, hope, and a future together, Rodger and Caroline Calvert walked toward their mansion on Heart Island.

Time travel will forever change the lives affected by the sundials, perhaps even yours.